Echoes of Andalucía

Richard C Pizey

Other titles by Richard C Pizey

Ripples

For updates and information on forthcoming publications
check online at
www.augmentedfifth.com

Echoes of Andalucía

Richard C Pizey was born in London and educated at the Nautical College Pangbourne.

After leaving college, Richard pursued a variety of courses including hotel management and catering, and electronic engineering and telecommunications, typically spending most of the time with more like-minded people in the art department of Colchester Technical College.

After a spell in Australia, constructing boilers, selling encyclopaedias and playing guitar with a rock band, he returned to London via life in Munich and Copenhagen, eventually taking up a career as a recording engineer. During thirty years of pushing faders in the studio profession, Richard also wrote scripts and jingles for radio and television commercials.

Having spent his childhood in exotic locations such as Bombay, Valletta, and Portsmouth (the UK version), and formative years in Australia, Germany and Denmark, it is perhaps little wonder that Richard still travels extensively. His interests include cosmology, tennis, music (especially classical and jazz funk), and wine.

Echoes of Andalucía is the second novel from author Richard C Pizey. His first novel, _Ripples,_ is available from bookshops or at www.augmentedfifth.com

Set in 14.5pt Garamond

ISBN 978 0 9566452 0 3

Printed in the UK by Copytech (UK) Limited

Echoes of Andalucía

Richard C Pizey

AUGMENTED FIFTH
ANOTHER DIMENSION

Pour   Francesca

Amie à vie, confidente et mentor sans pareille

Muchísimas gracias . . .

hasta la familia Ruiz Lopez
por su amistad y por su conocimiento inimitable
de Andalucía y su gente, y por enseñarme la estilo
de vida de l'Axarquia.

hasta Jorge Retana Alumbreros
por su ayuda inestimable con las rectificaciónes
en mi Español discutible.
(A glossary of Spanish words and phrases
as used in the novel is given on pages 239 - 243)
Any inaccuracies are mine, and mine alone.

. . . y, por último,
hasta Mirta Raquel Pintos, la princesa de Uruguay.
Muchísimas gracias por todo,
por la dirección con la idioma tuya,
y especialmente por tu sonrisa grande.
¿Y ahora, qué?

Contents:

1. Civil War

Onward and upward, onward and upward, the hill, unremitting, seemed interminable. Driving rain, whipped into horizontal fury by hurricane-force winds, lashed unmercifully at the three men as they struggled to make progress. Each tree they passed looked identical, a blur of twiggy outlines in stormy confusion. There was no way of knowing how far they'd travelled, only the pain from screaming calf-muscles told them they were making actual headway.

Onward and upward, onward and upward.

'Stop, stop,' José gasped. 'For Christ's sake, stop.'

Grinding to an undignified halt, he wiped the rain from his eyes and peered through turbulent weather. 'This is madness,' he panted, chest heaving with the strain of the climb. Aware of the heavy hammering of blood seething through veins and capillaries, and with the thud of an overworked heart echoing in his ears, he struggled to gain control of his breathing.

'Where are we, José? Where the hell are we?' Sebastián asked, hoping against hope his friend would have some idea.

José looked at him, saw the worry etched on his face, visible under the stubble, under the sheen of grimy sweat. 'Somewhere near Canillas,' he puffed. 'Must be.'

He paused to suck more air into his tortured lungs and leaned forward to rest his hands on his knees. 'Look,' he said, pointing downhill. 'Down there, that's the stream we've been following for the past couple of hours.' Each phrase was punctuated by laboured breathing. 'It continues past the village, through that valley towards its source in the mountains.'

The stream was a raging torrent, fed by a thousand gushing springs, a thousand rivulets as the surrounding hillsides tried to shake off the heavy mantle of water. It had been raining for twenty-four hours without let up, big heavy drops, shiny black pearls crashing down, relentless, out of leaden skies. There had been thunder and lightening as well, violent and vicious; bad enough during daytime but now, as sodden hours marched relentlessly towards evening, it was hell, the encroaching darkness rent asunder by the sudden brilliant fire of God. Temporarily blinding, it impeded their progress and gnawed at their already frayed nerves.

They'd come to a halt at the base of a rocky outcrop, a large chunk of splintered granite leaning at a crazy angle towards a solitary olive tree.

Manolo, the elder of the trio, shook his head and grinnned in damp desperation. Reaching into his jacket and beneath his shirt, from the armpit of a sweat-stained vest he produced a pack of cigarettes, and although battered and the worse for wear, the contents at least were dry. Fishing in his trouser pockets, he located a lighter, and opening his jacket as each man took one of the proffered cigarettes, brought the lighter into the relative calm and flicked the lever. As soon as José and

Sebastián were happily puffing away, Manolo bent his head forward and lit a cigarette for himself. Not only had the jacket been essential in that it allowed them to ignite their tobacco, it also provided a screen, concealing the flame from prying eyes.

It was a time of fear, a time when it was hard to trust anyone – neighbours, friends, family; trust was a rare sentiment these days. The civil war had been raging for eighteen months and had affected everyone. Beliefs and emotions ran deep and were strictly adhered to, there were few areas of murky grey. Individuals were protective about their tenets and the resulting chaos tore at the heart of the nation.

Old family feuds bubbled to the surface, virulent puss spewing from a seething cauldron, rending asunder the very fabric of humanity. Brothers had taken opposing sides, one denouncing the other, husbands and wives separated, families disappeared. Whole hamlets and villages ceased to exist, their inhabitants slaughtered by the malevolent jack-booted forces unleashed by Generalissimo Franco, the would-be king.

Desperately seeking respite from the ceaseless rain, the trio pressed their backs against the gnarled trunk of the ancient olive. It was no use. The deluge had caused the canopy of leaves to become as much use as a sieve, each gust of wind releasing a cascade of water from leaves and branches alike. Sliding under shirt collars, the rain, exuding coolness into perspiration, generated a hot foetid clamminess, plastering material to skin and effectively blocking the ingress of air, effectively raising the body temperature. The men were soaked and steaming.

A clatter of gunfire alerted them to the ever-present danger surrounding them on every side and, although distant, the noise was enough to warn them that the Nationalist guard was still systematically rampaging through the countryside, seeking out dissenters and insurgents. Throughout the day, sporadic fighting had broken out on the streets of Vélez-Málaga, snipers picking off anyone bold enough to leave the sanctuary of their home. In the madness of civil war it had become increasingly difficult to know who was fighting who, and chance encounters with strangers became experiences accompanied by nervous distrust, when ambiguity, more often than not, would be quickly resolved through instant death. The past week had witnessed the eastward march of rampant bloodshed, the army ruthlessly stamping out any pockets of resistance. Terror had been let loose and was stalking the coastline, Nationalist troops in their ridiculous up-turned helmets swarming like ants towards Almería.

After weeks of uncertainty, José, Manolo and Sebastián had had enough, no matter that they hadn't actually done anything wrong; apart of course from the night when they'd traipsed around town pasting up posters ridiculing the dictator's régime. It had been fun, dangerous fun, and the following day the three young men had observed the reactions of the townsfolk. The split had been fifty-fifty, supporters and antagonists, left and right, citizens spoiling for meltdown spurred on by rumours flooding the streets like ricocheting bullets. The three friends had decided to head for the hills and the relative safety of the mountains. They'd heard that the upland wilds were the hiding places of the resistance fighters, small groups of brave unsung heroes who were attempting to staunch Franco's mighty onslaught.

José turned to the others. 'Come on,' he said, 'we have to keep moving. We'll head further upstream, find a ruin or something, a cave or an overhang in the cliffs. We need better protection from this weather.'

Manolo and Sebastián, accepting unarguable reasoning, pinched the burning tobacco from half-smoked cigarettes and stashed them in inner pockets to await the next halt on their exodus from the coast into the mountains of Andalucía.

José had been right. Another forty-five minutes of hard, uphill trekking brought them into a narrow winding gorge, almost hidden beneath the village of Canillas de Albaida. Here, in deep green shadows, the tributary convulsed into another larger stream before passing beneath a footbridge, and the men thought of using the wooden crossing as a temporary refuge from the rain. They made their way down the steep ravine but found the torrent too strong, too dangerous. Rocks, branches and whole trees, picked up and swept along by tormented waters, thundered into the confluence, creating a maelstrom of frenzied confusion. The debris, hurling itself against the concrete foundations and metal supports of the small bridge, had become jammed and was starting to pile up. Frustrated, the trio scrambled back up the bank, crossed the bridge and continued to follow the track, which became progressively narrower the further upstream it led.

A few minutes later, Manolo broke into a run.

'Look, look,' he yelled, speeding ahead. 'A ruin.'

José and Sebastián, lumbering behind, followed him into the dilapidated stone building.

'This'll do,' said José, 'at least, for an hour or so.'

He looked back through the empty doorframe and was able to see as far as the bridge. 'Yep,' he said, 'this is fine, we can see, but we can't be seen. From here we can keep a lookout to cover our tracks in case anyone's been following.'

The construction was small, only about four-metres-by-three, and probably had once been a shelter for shepherds. The walls were more or less intact but the roof had collapsed inwards, leaving one end of the habitat with no protection from the elements. At the other end, however, there was some semblance of refuge. A jumble of wooden beams had fallen lengthways to the ground and with their upper ends wedged against the top of the walls, formed a slanting frame, a canopy of lichen-covered timber.

Crawling into the space under the sloping rafters, the three men at last found alleviation from the constant battering of rain. Huddled together, it wasn't long before they fell asleep, their fatigue manifest.

* * *

Careful not to rouse his slumbering companions, José crept from under the makeshift shelter and peered through the opening. The rain had ceased its furious downpour, the incessant roar replaced by an eerie silence, punctuated now and again as giant drops of water, sliding across leaves and branches, fell heavily into saturated ground.

Drawing the collar of his jacket tight around his neck, José ventured out of the ruin. He knew their situation was becoming desperate. Early the previous morning, they'd finished their meagre rations; stale bread and a sweating baton of salami having provided barely enough energy to see them through the rigours of the day. They needed to find provisions, now, before heading deeper into the uncertain realms of the high sierras.

Familiar with the area from times when his brother, a few years senior, had led him on exciting far-flung missions of discovery, José had decided upon a sneaky reconnaissance of the village at the top of the hill. Setting off at a brisk walk, he recrossed the bridge and started an uphill trek towards a dubious destination. From everywhere, came the sound of rushing water, unleashed rivulets swelling into gulleys becoming ever deeper and wider as the volume of water, obeying the laws of gravity, collected and divided. The track, often no more than a vaguely scored path marked here and there with goat droppings, was etched against the harsh landscape by an occasional moon, a small silver orb playing hide-and-seek with an assortment of storm-tossed clouds.

Grimly determined, José plodded on, automatically placing one foot in front of the other until, rounding a corner, he came upon a section of path that had almost disappeared, demolished and replaced by the loose scree of a recent landslide. Like a spider investigating the supportiveness of a broken web, he gingerly traversed the unstable slurry of mud, rock and broken trees, each step an advance into the unknown. It took three minutes to reach stable ground, although to José it seemed an eternity. One pace, another pace, a pause to listen to dislodged pebbles tumbling onto the rocks fifty metres below; with each hesitant step, he wondered if he too was about to slide away into the oblivion of instant death.

An hour after starting out from the relative safety of the ruin, he was relieved to find the path gradually levelling out. Winding through a stand of skimpy pines, it led past a whitewashed low-level barn before decending onto the main street via a series of steps worn into a rocky slope

It was about ten-thirty, certainly no later than eleven, and the place appeared to be deserted. Unable to discern any glimmer of light, José kept close to the sheltering houses and set off along the narrow lane, following its gentle upward slope until he came to the bakery. Peering around the corner, he saw a sliver of pale-yellow light gleaming across slick flagstones, perhaps a hundred metres distant.

Able to boast only two streets, one colliding into the other at something approaching a right angle, the village, since inception, had been pushing at limited boundaries. Lumped together on either side of the narrow streets, the huddle of buildings featured crudely designed extensions in any and every possible direction. Through generations of haphazard construction, additional oblongs and rectangles had sprouted in random multiplicity, rather in the manner of wooden blocks being arranged by some bored four-year-old. This gave everything the impression of being joined together and made it difficult to know where one house ended before seemingly flowing into the next.

Cautiously, José made his way towards the slender beam of light, realizing as he approached that it was sliding through a crack beneath an ill-fitting door. Before getting too close, he paused, straining to hear a sound, a noise, any hint that might give warning of the proximity of inhabitants. There was nothing, only silence. Silence from the street and silence from within the house.

Discovering the door to be partially open, he craned his head around the jamb and became aware of heat emanating from a small parlour. He eased the door a little wider, and on seeing that the room was deserted, entered quickly and scanned the sparsely furnished interior. One corner was occupied by a large upholstered armchair and, next to it, a small stubby wood burner, gently exhaling comforting clouds of smoky warmth. A table and two chairs, angled obliquely, stood next to the wall opposite the door, and a sideboard, supporting Christ on a cross and a photograph of someone in uniform, completed the visual itinerary. Peering more closely at the table, José wondered at a piece of linen carelessly draped over three or four bulky objects, objects that begged investigation. In two strides he crossed the room, removed the cloth and found salvation – a *jamon*,[1] some bread, a jug of milk and a watermelon.

The decision, made in a split second, was easy. José opened his shoulder bag and rapidly transferred the haunch of ham, the bread and the watermelon, from table to knapsack. He tied the cord at the top of the bag, slung it over his shoulder and hastened out of the room. Looking neither left nor right, he kept his head down and retraced his steps along the silent street. After only a few paces, he felt something brush against the side of his head, a sensation that caused him to stop in his tracks. He turned and found himself staring into the eyes of an upside-down face. 'Jesus,' he muttered through clenched teeth.

Looking up, he saw a body suspended by its feet, a thick rope, wrapped securely around the ankles, leading up to a metal rail bordering a balcony six or seven metres above street level. The man's hands had been pulled behind his back and fastened by means of a thin cord, gravity causing the arms to hang away from his body at an unnatural angle.

José took an unsteady pace backwards and at the same instant, the moon, sliding from behind a cloud, bathed the macabre spectacle in ghostly light. He moved his attention back to the man's face and couldn't help but notice the ragged gash beneath the chin, running from ear to ear. Blood from the vicious wound had run down both sides of the man's face and into his hair, shaping it into shiny downward pointing spikes, a hairstyle created in crimson death.

José looked up and down the street, it was empty, he was alone with the spectacle in front of him – an upside-down body, murdered and suspended in space, surrounded by silence and illuminated by a fitful moon – a scene dragged from a nightmare. He wondered where were the people who had committed this atrocity and, swearing to himself, cursed the war and cursed his own countrymen for being so stupid, faction fighting faction with no end in sight, only more misery, more pain, and more death. He crossed himself and moved away, heading towards the little path that would lead him from this hideous pointlessness.

Navigating the corner by the baker's shop, he stumbled into a pile of crates, causing several of them to clatter onto the stone-flagged street. Certain that the noise would attract attention from curious villagers, José froze and stood stock-still. A minute passed, then two, and no one appeared. Clambering over the collapsed heap, he was moved by sudden inspiration and, grabbing a crate in each hand, ran back to the hanging man. Balancing one crate on top of the other, he climbed on to them and by standing on tiptoe was able to reach the rope tethering the body to the railings. He pulled his knife from a sheath attached to his belt and in one rapid slice, severed the leash. The corpse, crashing down onto the crates, knocked José off his perch and the two bodies hit the ground simultaneously. Without pausing to think or look about him, José hauled the inert body up and over his shoulder and staggered towards the bakery.

Step by laboured step, he forced himself to continue, his burden becoming heavier with every movement. Turning past the shop, he began to zigzag up the rock face, carefully placing his feet into each tread until at last he reached the barn. Locating a small wooden door, he kicked it open, allowing himself a smile when the wood splintered under the force of his booted foot. The barn was empty – no goats, no sheep, no pigs – and the roof was too low to accommodate an animal the size of a horse.

Laying the body on the straw-covered floor, he used his knife to cut the cord binding the man's hands. Working quickly, he scraped aside some of the straw, rolled the body into the cleared space and folded the man's arms across his chest. Looking at the corpse, inert on the cold stone floor, José shook his head and once again crossed himself before covering the dead body with handfuls of straw.

Happy to have done something to avenge or at least surprise the people who had carried out the slaughter, he backed out through the broken door, pulled it shut, and resumed his trek down the mountainside. His body drenched in sweat, José was glad to be heading downhill, and as he walked and stumbled along the rough track, he thought about the war and the countless thousands who had lost their lives fighting for the cause – the bloody stain that was creeping throughout his beloved country. Railing at the futility of war and the sheer stupidity of man, he became aware of tears crowding his eyes, and every once in a while he kicked out angrily at the small rocks and pebbles littering the path. He despised the belligerence of "Miss Canary Islands", the pint-sized dictator, but above all, he cursed his own desperation and helplessness.

Eventually, reaching the little wooden bridge and wary that his colleagues, if awake, might think him to be the enemy, José began to creep stealthily towards the ruin.

*   *   *

'You're covered in blood,' Sebastián cried in alarm, pointing at José's jacket. 'Look! It's all over you.'

The three were sitting on some large boulders, a group of rocks scattered at random across a small meadow stretched between the ruin and the hectic stream. The sun was shining from a cloudless sky, flies buzzed around their heads, and the only tell-tale signs of the previous day's storm, came from the noise of roaring water in the engorged stream and the occasional resounding crack of uprooted trees being hurled against the unyielding constriction of the bridge.

'Mmm,' José agreed, opening his shoulder bag and unveiling the stolen victuals.

'Food!' Sebastián exclaimed, as bread, ham and watermelon were set out on one of the boulders. 'Who did you have to kill to get that?'

'He was already dead,' José answered. 'And it wasn't *his* food in any case, at least I don't suppose it was.'

'But, where . . ?'

'Up there in the village, Canillas,' José explained, using the shortened form of the village's name.

There was another Canillas about thirty kilometres to the west, Canillas de Aceituno, but round these parts the locals referred to both villages as Canillas. There was never any doubt as to which was which, thirty kilometres was a distance to be reckoned with and so far as these indigenes were concerned, Canillas de Aceituno might as well have been in a different country.

'A village? Up there?' Sebastián asked.

'A very small village, only two streets. An empty village, no people,' José told him.

'No people?' Sebastián queried. 'But the blood, the food, how . . ?'

'One dead person, strung up, hanging from a balcony. That's where the blood came from . . . I cut him down.'

'Jesus,' Sebastián said.

'Yeah,' José agreed, nodding, 'Jesus; only he's not doing too much to stop this shitty war.'

Each man produced a knife and while they set to work cutting up and dividing the food, José told them about his night-time expedition to the village.

Twenty minutes later and with stomachs full, they lit cigarettes, drawing on them heavily.

'Seems we'd better get away from here as soon as possible,' Manolo said, exhaling grey tobacco smoke towards his friends. 'Where do you suppose those villagers are?'

'No idea,' José replied, 'but they're going to be as mad as hornets. Not only has their corpse disappeared, they've also been robbed of some of their provisions.'

'Maybe it wasn't such a good idea?' Manolo suggested. 'Yeah, the food was necessary, but . . . moving the body?'

'Until I fell over those crates,' José explained, 'I hadn't thought about it. But . . . I was so pissed off, you know? It's one thing to kill someone, it's something else to hang 'em upside-down. It was a chance to strike back, an opportunity; I took it, that's all.' He collected the remaining food and stuffed it back into his satchel. 'Come on then, let's make a move.'

Following the right-hand fork of the stream, the going was difficult, and when the winding path led suddenly beneath swollen waters, they had to climb above the level of the rushing torrent and seek a way over the rocks and boulders edging the steep sided valley. Later, negotiating a curve to the north, they came across vegetation more dense, almost jungle-like – giant cactus plants, eucalyptus, oleander and scrubby bushes forming a barrier, making their passage more hazardous and hindering progress.

After a few metres of fighting through the undergrowth, José called a halt. 'Either we continue trying to follow the course of the stream,' he said, shaking his head, 'or we start climbing.'

'What happens if we climb?' Manolo asked.

'I don't know,' José replied, 'but it has to be easier than forcing our way through this stuff.'

'Where are we?' asked Sebastián.

'Nowhere special,' José answered. 'If we start climbing and keep heading north, we'll have to cross over these mountains and that'll bring us to Alhama . . . eventually, or maybe Játar.'

'Well . . . which?' Manolo asked, wiping sweat from his forehead.

'Depends. We'll probably come out somewhere in-between,' José said.

'Okay, let's go,' Sebastián said, deciding for them. 'When we get the other side of these mountains we can choose whether it's to be Alhama or Játar. Right now we need to keep moving.'

Turning their backs on the stream, they headed higher into the Sierra de Tejeda. The going should have become easier as they climbed out of the valley and left the trees and bushes behind them, but the ascent was relentless and it wasn't long before the men came to a halt.

'What I wouldn't give for coffee and *churros*,'[2] Manolo announced brightly, grinning at his companions.

'Come on,' said Sebastián, 'we can't afford to hang around. The army can't be far behind, neither can those murderous bastards from the village.'

'Just a minute,' José gasped. 'Let me get my breath back.'

Standing on the edge of the steep hillside, the trio paused for a couple of minutes and looked back in the direction from which they'd come. The stream was just visible, winding its way along the valley until it turned to the west and disappeared out of sight. There was no sign of any movement, no sign of any army and, more importantly, no group of irate people they thought might have been rampaging close on their footsteps.

After a while, they continued their uphill exodus. In places, the ascent was almost vertical and the three men found themselves searching for anything to cling onto, a clump of brittle fennel, a tuft of wide-bladed grass; or into, the tiniest fissure, a crack no greater than the depth of a shadow, any gap large enough to accommodate a fingernail.

It took them almost an hour to wrestle their way two hundred metres further up the mountainside, until at last the gradient became a little less aggressive. Ahead of them, a pine forest stretched across the face of progress, two dense tracts of booding obscurity separated by a breath of acrimonious rock. With Manolo in the lead, they plunged headlong into the dank interior, following a narrow path that wound back and forth through the maze of slender trees.

It was a different world, curiously silent, a secret arbour inhabited by the denizens of dark places – martens, foxes, wild boar, vipers; and visited occasionally by deer and freely roaming black bulls, undisputed kings of the mountain realms. Concentrating on the path's tortuous contortions, the men exchanged few words, and with footfalls deadened by countless layers of fallen pine needles and the sound of strained breathing absorbed by the fastness of the forest, the trio proceeded stealthily through eclipsed continuum.

Emerging suddenly into brilliant sunshine, they dithered on the periphery of an open expanse of rock-scattered highland. They'd reached the watershed, a ridge running the length of the Tejeda and marking the border between the provinces of Málaga to the south and Granada to the north. The air, washed clean by the previous day's rain, was heavily laden with the fragrance of wild herbs – thyme, rosemary, oregano and wild mint.

José, Sebastián and Manolo settled down with their backs to the westerly wind and shared between them the remnants of the plundered food. Enjoying the warm sunshine they took the opportunity to relax, and it was only a matter of minutes before they started talking about the subject uppermost on their minds, indeed, the subject that was *the* topic of conversation throughout the peninsula.

'Where's it all going to end?' Sebastián asked, looking from one glum face to the other. 'I mean, the country's falling apart at the seams. Just how long can this bloody war continue?'

Manolo shoved a large wedge of bread into his mouth and shook his head. 'It's all gone to shit,' he said, speaking around the ball of food. 'The country's gone to shit.'

'Yeah, I know,' José nodded, 'it certainly looks that way, but all the same there has to be something to hold on to, some small glimmer of hope.'

'Hope,' Sebastián growled, 'sometimes just isn't enough.'

'It is when there's nothing else,' José countered. 'I mean, look at us for example. Me?' he smacked himself on the chest, 'I'm liberal . . . so what? I want to defend democracy against Fascism, I want land redistribution and better conditions for everybody, especially here in the south where unemployment is out of control. And look at the church,' he continued, paraphrasing something his father had been talking about only the other day, 'the power of religion is too strong . . . and as for the Nationalist creed "destroy democracy", well, that just scares me rigid. Anyway, whatever, it's a fact; war is war, bloody, reckless and totally cazy. You know it, I know it, we all know it. We talk about it, we argue about it, we . . .' he smiled and looked at Manolo. '*You*, get angry and upset, but hell, we're still together, still the best of friends running through the shit that's all around us. Yes, it's true, we have different opinions and different beliefs, yet we're able to rise above them and maintain our friendship.'

He stopped, looked at the ground beneath his feet and thought about what he'd just said, thinking back to their schooldays and the tiny village school where they'd forged their camaraderie, their respect for one another, he and Manolo; but Manolo, in his head, had opted for the rebels and labelled himself a Carlist. José shook his head at the absurdity of it all. Left and Right, Republicans and Nationalists, the country was divided, the schism unbridgeable.

'Franco is strong,' Manolo ventured. 'He'll pull the country together, get it on its feet in the same way that Hitler is doing with Germany.'

'By killing everyone who disagrees with him?' José asked. 'The Spanish Inquisition is alive and well.'

'Wait until the African Army gets here,' Manolo said haughtily. 'That'll sort everything out. We'll have law and order in no time.'

'Just as well, then, that the navy came out on the Republican side,' José rejoined. 'Without ships, the troops'll stay stuck in Morocco.'

'I don't like it,' Sebastián said, summing up his feelings, 'it's all too dangerous. Look, it's not just artists, writers and intellectuals fleeing in droves, it's everybody. What's going to become of our country?'

The friendship had blossomed and expanded to encompass Sebastián when, in nineteen-thirty-four after the brutal defeat of the October revolution, he and his family had moved from Cudillero in the extreme north of the country, to the extreme south – Asturias to Andalucía.

Despite adhering to differing ideals regarding the future of their divided country, the three had managed to maintain their relationship, placing it at a level far removed from the infantile pettiness of politics. In José's own family however, the civil war and its attendant follies had led almost to the unforgivable act of fratricide, endemic to countless families riven in two, many finding themselves simply in the wrong place at the wrong time.

'It may take a while,' José said, summing up his feelings, 'but I think the struggle will wear itself out, eventually.'

'What makes you say that?' Manolo asked.

'It has to,' José replied. 'People have to realize the stupidity of it all, the useless waste of lives. They have to start living together, you know, like us? Someone has to make a start, to stand up and be counted. The people of Spain, the ordinary everyday people who care about their country, they should forget the politics and ignore the politicians that got us into this mess.'

'Yeah,' Manolo agreed, 'show me a politician and I'll show you a waste of space.'

'*¡Joder!*[3] there you go again,' José grinned, cuffing his friend on the shoulder, 'but you're right, I a*gree*, all of them, Manolo, they're complete idiots. Armed with basic intelligence and an unbridled passion for power, what else could they be? And what sort of power do they end up with? Corruptive political power, nothing more, nothing less; exploitation by one class over another. And that's not power, it's tyranny.' He paused, collecting his thoughts. 'Ultimately, they're responsible for all this bloodshed.'

'Makes a change from religion,' Sebastián said, giggling. 'Hell, we should form an oligarchy. Right here, right now.'

'Yes, we should,' the others agreed in unison.

'An oligarchy of three,' José grinned. 'Hmm, something like the Holy Trinity.'

'Something like the Unholy Trinity,' Manolo pointed out.

'That's it,' Sebastián said, 'humour, the answer to all mankind's problems. Hell,' he continued, 'we should have some wine to make a toast.' Penknife in hand, he lifted it into the air like a miniature sword, sunlight glinting on the greasy blade. 'Here's to humour!'

'Bollocks to that,' Manolo said. 'We should have some wine to make a toast to our*selves*.' He raised the haunch of ham above his head. 'Here's to the Unholy Trinity!'

'Sorry,' José apologized. 'The house in Canillas was fresh out of wine.'

The conversation was over, the sting temporarily removed from the poisonous theme.

'Why can't it work for everyone?' José asked himself, as the three men returned to the serious task of eating their meal. He was fifteen, going on sixteen, tall, strong and willowy, and regarded by the others as leader, even though Manolo was two years his senior. He looked at his friends – teenagers, youngsters become adults at an early age – and wondered about the future; in the madness of civil war, normality had ceased to exist, a consequence being deprivation of youth. Then he started wondering about his brother, a staunch supporter of the Nationalist cause, glued to his principles and stuck in Madrid.

José lifted his eyes to focus instead on the beauty that surrounded him. To the south, the view was magnificent, encompassing mountains and valleys shelving away to the Mediterranean sparkling in the distance, a natural extension of the sky. The sea's azure depths painted a broad bold brush-stroke across the blue horizon against which, the hills – some jagged, some rounded with verdant crowns – formed stark silhouettes. The lucid atmosphere, vibrant with crystal clarity, permitted visibility so intense as to be almost painful, it seemed possible to see forever. Torre del Mar, a tiny fishing village, was easily visible, as was the coastline stretching westwards towards another small village, Fuengirola, far distant across the bay of Málaga.

To the north, the mountains dipped towards the plains, a landscape of arable countryside blending into precise olive groves, marshalled ranks of dark-brown gnarled limbs shimmering in late September sunshine, row upon row stretching into infinity, connecting Andalucía to the deep red interior of Castilla-la Mancha, home to white-washed windmills and the ghosts of Sancho and brave Don Quixote. In the distance, the deep wound of the gorge winding around the feet of the perilous cliffs of Alhama de Granada could be seen snaking through the volcanic defile, a place of sulphur-laden springs.

Rested and replete, it was time to move on.

'Where to?' asked Manolo.

'It's all downhill,' José answered, pointing northwards. 'Just there, look, those broken peaks . . . see? Those are known as the "Bad Beds". If we skirt round to the west and then keep heading in a northerly direction, we should just about clear the foothills by nightfall.'

'Then what?' Manolo demanded.

'Don't know,' said José. He looked at his two friends. 'I suppose we just have to keep on going.'

'But . . . where?'

'I don't know,' José repeated. 'We need to find somewhere safe,' he added, grinning ruefully, 'but that might be just about impossible. The country has been torn apart and trust is a thing of the past, especially for three strangers who turn up out of nowhere. And now that that bastard Generalissimo has teamed up with Hitler and his fat friend Mussolini, there's no knowing where it'll end.'

He picked up his shoulder bag, now empty, and set off across the rocky divide, leading his friends toward an uncertain future.

* * *

Damp, dark and cold, the cave had provided some form of refuge for the three men.

The march across rough terrain had taken longer than expected, the rain of the previous two days having turned all the streams into raging torrents. A few had proved impassable, necessitating a tramp along their winding courses in order to find some location a little more accessible. The excursions were frequent and dangerous, and sometimes the streams would disappear over the edge of a precipice, leaving the travellers no option but to turn around and follow the swollen waters in the opposite direction. Progress was painfully slow and each time an obstacle was successfully negotiated, the resultant euphoric sense of achievement was pathetically short-lived.

It was after one such crossing that they'd discovered the cave, literally by falling into it. Rolling over the upper periphery, they'd clattered and banged against one another until coming to an undignified halt at the back of the hollow. After a few moments spent untangling themselves, the relief at finding they'd survived, save for a few cuts and bruises, caused them to sit and giggle like a bunch of halfwits.

'We might as well stay here,' José suggested.

He walked the few paces to the opening and became silhouetted against the deepening night. Turning back to his colleagues, he told them, 'Might not be so lucky next time.'

There had been no argument. All three were aware of the dangers that a night-time traverse of this mountainous area would entail, a twisted ankle or a broken leg would be the least of their worries. José and Manolo knew the region, they'd lived and breathed it all their lives and were well acquainted with the sudden scarps and sliding screes, and paid due respect to the treacherous low branches of the olives and almonds, which at night-time became wild Hydra, catching, ripping and tearing at unwary travellers.

'Come on, let's . . .' José's idea was cut short. 'Fuck!' he said, tripping over some unknown obstacle. Flinging out a hand, he touched something soft and furry. 'What's this?' he asked, voice shaky. 'It's . . . a sheep. Wait, no . . . it's . . . it's a goat!' He chuckled, quickly forgetting the few seconds of paralysed anxiety. 'Must've played the same trick we did, not watching where it was putting its feet. Unusual for a goat.' He laughed, releasing tension, 'But, these are unusual times.'

A short while later, José, Sebastián and Manolo were huddled happily and cosily around a hastily constructed fire, swapping stories and watching chunks of butchered goat bubble and blister, gobbets of melted fat dripping down to hiss madly on the glowing pile of timbers. The meal that evening was something of a feast, a God-sent celebration, and again the three friends lamented the lack of a decent drink – a beer or a glass of wine. Night deepened and conversation stumbled into introspection. And when at last the dying embers dulled into vagueness, exhaustion gave way to sleep.

The next morning started grey and murky, and one by one, the men exited the cave and disappeared into thick hanging mist.

'It's creepy,' Sebastián whispered over his shoulder. In the lead and hearing no answer, he stopped and waited for Manolo to catch up. 'Creepy,' he repeated.

'Eerie,' Manolo agreed, wiping cold moisture from his face.

Five seconds later, José bumped into them. 'Why have we stopped?' he asked.

'It's pretty weird,' Sebastián started, trying to explain the halt. 'The mist deadens everything. It's so quiet, I can't even hear your footsteps.'

'Probably 'cause I'm not moving,' José observed.

'You know what I mean,' Sebastián told him, when suddenly, the mist dissolved into a myriad of sparkling droplets, each one swirling away under the influence of an emergent sun.

'Magic!' Manolo remarked, observing the transformation. 'Such power, such beauty, such . . .'

'Such a romantic,' Sebastián told him.

'Yeah? Well, you should know, coming from the north,' Manolo responded.

'What do you mean by that?' Sebastián asked.

'All that rain, all those forests, everything green . . .'

'As opposed to these barren mountains?' Sebastián countered.

'Too much rain,' Manolo expounded. 'Makes the brain go mushy.'

'And mushiness produces poetry?' José queried, drawn into the argument.

'Apparently,' Sebastián agreed, grinning at his comrades and putting an end to the superficial quid pro quo.

Trailing along astern of his companions, José found himself falling into realms of improbability, found himself nurturing unwholesome, unwelcome thoughts. The odyssey was beginning to take on the aspects of a dream, a nightmarish descent into the world of Sisyphus. The journey was fraught with unseen danger, dark forces manoeuvring behind them, in front of them, and all around them, and now that the mist had evaporated, José couldn't help but look about, nervously expecting each tree, each rock, each clump of tall waving grasses, to turn into a paradigm of death. No matter what they did, no matter where they went or to whom they turned in this God-forsaken country, José and his friends would forever be struggling against impossible odds.

The afternoon, like the journey, had been long. Uncertain and enervating, it had stretched ahead of the weary travellers, beckoning them towards ever-new horizons which proved mercifully to be uneventful. Since gravitating from higher ground they'd found the going slightly easier, but still had to be wary of the recently cut deep gullies. At last they came to the edge of a gently sloping valley, in the centre of which stood a ramshackle collection of buildings, desolate and precariously held together by a whim of nature.

It was evening, and the weather had reverted to an arrangement of squally showers. The light, fading rapidly under heavy layers of cloud, turned vision into guesswork, and the trio, positioned behind a thicket of prickly shrubs, peered cautiously into gathering shadows.

They could see no sign of movement from the area around the dilapidated buildings, but . . . they couldn't be too careful. Earlier in the afternoon, when they'd been higher up in the foothills, they'd come upon a herd of goats grazing happily on scraggy brush and tufts of grass growing haphazardly amongst the rocky outcrops. There had been no fencing, no corral, and no attendant shepherd, the goats content to wander unsupervised, scavenging what they could from the sparse vegetation.

'What do you reckon?' José asked, after they'd spent some time studying the lie of the land.

'Seems okay,' Sebastián said. 'Looks deserted; maybe just a shepherd, maybe no-one.'

'Mmm,' José agreed.

They stood up, José and Sebastian, and a shot rang out. Explosive cacophony. The noise creased harshly through the damp curtain of dusk, a brief flicker of light sliding from a cold dark metal tube. Both men clawed at their throats, both men felt their fingers sliding through thick red viscosity. Both men screamed.

Sebastián, dying, fingertips groping around his shattered larynx, fell to the ground.

José, startled, sheets clinging to his clammy body, opened his eyes.

2. Breakfast

It was the way she smacked her wooden stick against the bed-room door. Every morning it was the same thing, the crack of wood against wood. José opened his mouth before realizing he had nothing to say.

'Come on you lazy old bugger, get out of bed.'

María's morning greeting, unnecessarily breezy, grated through the atmosphere and stimulated José's sluggish neu-rons. Never was there any variation. Fifty-five years of mar-riage, horse and carriage harnessed and dancing the same dance, the same daily ritual; marionettes, following closely the parameters set by rote and etched firmly into their lives.

María swished across the bedroom and peeled back the curtains. 'Look, half the day gone already,' she said turning round, forming a dark outline against the bright radiance of the world outside.

José blinked as strong unfiltered sunlight swept in through the window, spotlighting the never ceasing interplay of free-fall dust motes. 'Half the day?' he muttered, glaring at the large-faced alarm clock. 'What do you mean, "half the day"? It's only half-past eight.'

'Precisely,' María, snarled at him. 'Then it's nine, then it's half-past nine, then ten, and before you know where you are, it's midday.'

José shook his head in amazement, wondering at his wife's perspicacity.

'Well?' María said, hands on hips, challenging.

José threw back the sheet and manoeuvered himself to the edge of the small timber-framed bed. He yawned and scratched his belly while his feet described lazy patterns on the stone floor, searching for his slippers.

María turned on her heels, walked across the room and ducked through the low doorway separating the bedroom from the kitchen. José, drawing his dressing gown around his torso, shuffled along after her. The effort of moving woke him just enough to find his voice and engage his brain.

'What's for breakfast?' he demanded.

'"What's for breakfast?"' María said, mimicking. 'Every morning you ask the same old question and every morning you get the same old answer, and today . . . it's the same as always.'

'What is?'

'Breakfast,' María replied, exasperated.

José's place at the rectangular wooden table had been set with a plate, a mug, a knife and a spoon. In fact, it had been done the night before – it was the custom, María's custom. She liked to lay the table before going to bed, throwing a clean white cloth over the scratched wooden surface and setting out the cutlery, two settings, one for her and one for him. Today being Thursday, José found his plate, mug and cutlery resting directly on top of the scrubbed table. It was laundry day, and the tablecloth, along with a blouse and one of José's tatty old shirts, was already soaking in warm soapy water in the tub outside the front door.

María pulled at the kitchen chair, its legs scraping against the floor, and left it in its new position so that José could slouch onto it. Lowering his sleepy weight onto the polished wooden seat, he dragged it forwards until his legs took up residence under the table. He looked down at the surface and inspected the layout of cutlery, noticing that María's place, as always, was devoid of implements, a few crumbs providing sole attestation to the frugal meal she'd consumed two hours earlier.

Placing his hands on the table, José inadvertently moved his knife, causing it to knock against the spoon, and the resultant metallic *'ting'* gleefully accompanied the sound of porcelain against porcelain as María placed a bowl of steaming porridge onto the plate in front of her husband.

It was all part of the ritual. José loved his porridge; it was, as his mother used to say, "the food of kings, stuff that made men out of boys". From as far back as he could remember, every day had begun with porridge; sun or rain, summer or winter, his mother, and now his wife, would place a bowlful of hot soggy oats in front of him.

María picked up the jug of goat's milk and poured a generous amount onto the warm sticky gloop, leaving José to administer the sugar, four spoonfuls of white gritty granules. His arthritis was worse this morning, and faltering dexterity caused some of the sugar to miss the target and form a concentric pattern on the tabletop, outlining precisely the curve of the plate.

He was hungry, he was always hungry, and María would spend great chunks of the day preparing food to place in front of her ever expanding, ever shrinking husband. He was expanding outwards – 'billowing' was the word María liked to use when gossiping with the women in the village – and shrinking earthwards. José was developing into a caricature of Buddha, the man with the belly, a large rotundity balanced on two spindly legs. In actuality it was three spindly legs, two real ones and a wooden stick which José used whenever it was necessary to perambulate more than a few paces.

José's stick had become his constant companion, and for a number of years it was as though his body had grown a new appendage. He used it to scratch at the dusty ground when trying to calculate his age; he used it to emphasize an issue, to mark out a boundary, to indicate a direction; and he used it to beat the dogs that seemed forever to hang about the *cortijo*.[4] It was José's trusty servant and wherever José went, the stick went too. It accompanied him to the pub, the shop, and the lavatory, and whenever he sat talking with the men in the plaza, the stick became the vital accessory which, when propped under his chin, prevented his drowsy head from collapsing onto his chest. María referred to it as José's "friend" and every time he exited the front door, the air would part to allow the words 'have you got your friend?' to catch up with him. José, of course, *always* had his "friend", it was part of him, manifest and essential.

José had always looked older than his actual age. When he was forty, he'd looked sixty, and when he was forty-five, he'd looked seventy. There had been nothing he could do about it, even had he considered doing so. His short stocky stature and dark, sun-ripened skin, betrayed his true age, and daily exposure to the heat and dust of Andalucía, served only to expedite the ageing process.

Years of hard toil and the grind of carrying heavy sacks – full of almonds in October and November and stuffed with olives in December and January – also had taken their toll. The sacks, weighing from fifty to sixty kilograms, were transported from tree to collection point on the harvesters' broad shoulders, and the resultant damage to overworked, overstretched limbs, was all too evident when observing the elderly men of the village, each fully kitted out with his 'friend', slowly and painfully making their way along the streets. Some would wave acknowledgement, a creaky 'Hola,' accompanied by the rickety waving of a stick, while others, minds focused on matters profound, would give no signal, no form of greeting as they prowled round the village locked into their own little worlds.

And then, they died, and were boxed up and placed in a hole in a wall forever to dream of their beloved mountains, their spirits free to inhabit the sun-baked slopes, to rest in the shade of an olive tree and capture the sweet musty scent of blossoming almonds.

With María fast approaching the table to collect the porridge bowl, José used his spoon to scrape the last vestiges of sticky substance from the sides and the bottom of the dish, then, having licked the spoon till it shone, he placed it back in the bowl and smiled sweetly. María removed the empty bowl with one hand and with the other, placed two thick slices of bread onto the plate – it was a deft movement, honed to perfection. Each slice had been toasted, rubbed with garlic and smothered under a generous coating of pulped tomato.

While José made inroads on the warm toast, María poured

some rich black coffee into his mug, and after pouring a mug for herself, went to lean against the sink. Holding the coffee between cupped hands, she sipped at the scalding brew and allowed herself to relax, thinking vaguely as she peered across the top of the mug at the lines etched deeply into José's face. The lines were moving erratically, facial muscles bunching and contracting, forming intricate patterns as José chewed on his toast. Although he never seemed to be certain of his age – somewhere around seventy, he'd tell people when asked – María knew exactly how old he was. He'd been born in December 1922 and, by María's reckoning, that put him at the grand old age of seventy-nine.

'I have to go to the shop,' she announced through wispy aromas of coffee. 'When I come back, you can help me wring out the washing.'

José nodded obediently and swallowed the last fragment of toast. Picking up his mug, he upended it and sent the dark brown liquid sluicing down his gullet, chasing its way after the sodden pellet of bread. María collected the used mug and plate, rinsed them under a stream of cold water and added them to the small pile of crockery waiting to one side of the deep porcelain sink.

'I'll wash these while I'm preparing lunch,' she informed the depths of the sink as much as informing José; he wasn't listening anyway, his mind occupied with plans for the rest of the day.

María stepped outside to prod at sodden clothing.

'José,' she called, trying to win his attention, at the same time drying her hands on her apron, her favourite threadbare apron. The ancient garment, decorated with little blue flowers on what once was a white background, now a uniform dull grey, was fastened by means of two frayed linen ties meeting in a large floppy bow somewhere behind María's tired body.

'Can't understand it, myself,' José said, enigmatic as ever. He raised his eyes from their scrutiny of the tabletop, aiming them at María as she scuttled back inside to remonstrate with her husband.

'What?' María asked.

'What?' José countered.

María's hands flew to their favourite resting place, balled fists on hips.

'What is it that you don't understand?' she asked, raising her voice several decibels to defeat the deafness suffered by her husband. Not only her husband, she thought suddenly, deafness was something inherent across virtually the whole Iberian Peninsula. It was hardly surprising, the noise levels throughout the land were astounding – restaurants with blaring televisions to which no one listened; cafés resonant with the stacking and restacking of crockery; and unchecked, un-baffled motor scooters roaring through narrow streets, engines amplified and echoing between rows of tiled houses. The population itself seemed intent on breaking the sound barrier. Whenever and wherever two or more people met, in a shop, in a bar, or on the pavements, they'd hurl sentences through the air at a volume designed to bring down the walls of Jericho. Maybe all this yelling and screaming was *because* of their deafness, María mused, smiling at the complexities of the home-grown paradox. She remembered reading an article in some paper or magazine – probably at the doctor's while waiting for José's prescriptions – that listed the noisiest countries in the world. Spain had been second on the list, while Japan, María seemed to recall, had been voted *numero uno*.

33

Removing her apron, she continued with her thoughts, wondering why it should be that Japan had been voted the noisiest place on the planet. She thought of the prim petite Japanese people and pictured their gardens, beautifully designed to give peace to the inner karma. She pondered on the grace of a geisha and the subtle fragrance of jasmine tea. Strange, she thought, her mind wandering through peaceful scenes, how a loud, brash, noisy modern Japan could be home to such picturesque serenity. She decided that the temples, pagodas, lotus blossoms and snow-capped mountains, must be the secret devices used by the slant-eyed islanders to attain their cherished tranquillity.

María returned to the bedroom and made the beds, an easy task requiring only the smoothing of a sheet and a shake, maybe two, to un-rumple the pillows. It was September and the nights were still warm although, at nearly six hundred metres, there was always a zephyr, the faintest of breezes carrying a sweet sensation of nectar as it whispered through the honeysuckle anchored to the latticework above the patio.

Turning from the beds, María stood in front of a heavy dark wooden chest, opened the top drawer and removed her black leather purse. It was well worn and bulged with the weight of the pesetas it struggled to contain. Back in the kitchen, she picked up her shopping-basket and headed out of the door. José had disappeared, but María guessed he'd be in the bathroom, performing his morning constitutional, regular as clockwork. Humming to herself and mentally going through the shopping-list, she set off down the little path.

José, having completed his daily ritual, ventured forth from the loo, leaving the creaky wooden door wide open so as to give the holy sepulchre of the porcelain throne a good airing. He rounded the corner, stepped onto the patio, and came face to face with María stepping onto the patio from the other direction. Having started on her way to the village, she'd walked only a few metres when she realized that she hadn't had an answer to her question. To María this was anathema, her questions always had to have answers.

José appraised his wife with a quizzical look.

'So, what is it that you don't understand?' María fired at him.

'Is this why you've come back so soon?'

'I need to know,' María said, standing firm. 'What don't you understand?'

'I don't understand why you get up so early,' José replied.

'Huh, to clean up after you,' María told him. 'It's a full-time occupation.'

'Is this not something you can do during the rest of the day?' José asked, hinting at a logically defined way of life.

'As well as the shopping, as well as feeding the dogs, the cats, feeding you, white-washing the house, cooking, doing the laundry, doing the ironing, putting the clean clothes away? Hmm, maybe it's something I should think about.'

María shook her head and began retracing her steps towards the village.

José, shaking his head to clear it from the burst balloon of logic, yelled 'Get a paper' after María's receding figure, and went into the kitchen.

After the glaring brilliance of the sun, the interior of the house was similar to a dimly lit cavern. José, however, knew the whereabouts of important features and manipulated his three legs to bring himself to the fridge. Removing a can of beer, he groped a hand across the top of ridiculously tall appliance and discovered a copy of last week's newspaper. Slamming shut the fridge door and causing everything to rattle, he returned to the patio and took up residence in his favourite chair.

In its position, backed up against the wall of the *cortijo*, the leather armchair was old and had seen better days. As with most of the furniture, it had been brought to the house many years ago on the back of a mule and deposited on the patio, where it had remained ever since. Having moulded itself to the exact outline of José's bulk, it was, to say the least, extremely comfortable. No matter that the stuffing was hanging out of several holes or that the leather, complete with rips and tears from the claws of generations of cats and dogs, had the appearance of an elderly Vietnamese pot-bellied pig, and no matter that one of the front corners was propped on a telephone directory, this was José's chair, José's seat of power.

It was known throughout the neighborhood that at any time of day, José could be found *here* in his place of refuge, his place of meditation, his seat of judgement. When people came to call, it was from here that José would hold court, dishing out advice on local problems, worldly problems, medical problems and problems of the heart. Stick in hand, José would become Thucydides, Ptolemy, Aristotle and Einstein; he had a view on everything, great or small, and was not shy about airing his opinions. Friends and relations referred to him as the "Oracle" and would organize trips to the little whitewashed *cortijo* in the mountains, where they'd sit in a semi-circle around the old leather armchair and listen to the pearls of wisdom issuing from the elder's mouth.

Sometimes, in the manner of wise men, the visitors would bring gifts – plastic water bottles full of home-produced wine, honey, a haunch of ham, a can or two of lager, some olives drowning in a secret home-evolved marinade, or maybe some cheese, or goat's milk. Always given a warm welcome, the guests would be greeted with a smile, a twinkle of the eyes and a shake of the hand before being told, *'Siéntense'*.[5] They would then sit in the aforementioned arc and while María fussed about producing drinks and platefuls of food, they'd wallow in the sea of information radiating towards them like ripples across a pond. During the summer months these sessions would continue long into the night, loose informal gatherings, discussions and conversations; variations on a theme compiled and processed while moths and mosquitoes fell prey to the snapping pink jaws of busy geckoes.

A large black fly buzzed angrily around José's head as he opened the paper and, for the hundredth time, started to read about the heinous crime that had been committed on distant American soil. It had happened last week, on Tuesday, and the world was still reeling, still replaying and reprinting those horrifying images of aircraft flying into the World Trade Center.

* * *

José, as usual, had been dozing on that warm September afternoon, safely secure in another time, another place, until María had come running up the path on her return from the village.

'José, José,' she'd called, the urgency in her voice dragging him suddenly back to the here and the now. She collapsed onto one of the plastic chairs that were always strewn around the patio. 'José, something terrible, *terrible!*'

José took a sip of beer from the can resting on the arm of

the armchair, spluttered as he spat out a fly. 'What?'

'Oh, José, something so awful, horrible. It's unbelievable.'

'Goodness sake woman, what?' he put the can of beer on the table, spilling a few drops in the process of reaching out of his chair.

'Passenger planes have crashed into those tall buildings in America,' María splurted out, trying to regain her breath. 'It's all over the telly, it's on every channel.'

'What tall buildings, where?' José asked, wondering what on earth could be the problem.

'Don't know,' María puffed, hands on knees, face the colour of beetroot.

'*Joder mujer,*[6] what *are* you talking about?' José insisted.

'It's on the telly, José. You'll see.'

He picked up his stick and prodded at the knob on the front of the ancient television set that had spent its entire life on the rickety table adjacent to José's seat of power. While electricity surged along antique cables and through dusty circuits to feed the large valves that then had to think about warming themselves up, it took forever before any picture was permitted to appear on the screen. Eventually, María and José were connected to the outside world and scenes of utter devastation were beamed live across the sleepy sunny terrace, where marigolds and geraniums jostled each other in crowded earthenware pots. Open mouthed, husband and wife watched as the drama unfolded in front of their eyes.

'Terrorists, damn terrorists,' José yelled at the little rectangle of animated glass.

'How do you know?' María asked, hands clasped in front of her mouth as she remained glued to the report from New York.

'Gotta be,' José replied. 'One plane it's an accident, two planes it's deliberate, an act of war.'

José had his opinions and they were strong, but at that precise moment, similar opinions were being echoed all around the planet. He sat with his stick resting across his legs and used the palms of his hands to roll it backwards and forwards as he took in the spectacle unfolding before him.

'Another beer,' he demanded. It was his way; platitudes and the finer aspects of etiquette were for others – the *beau monde* of Paris or Vienna, and, José grudgingly admitted to himself, the patricians of Madrid. He watched María's shadow pass in front of the television screen as she moved towards the kitchen. 'And bring something to eat,' he shouted after her.

He increased the downward pressure on the cane, felt it rubbing against the sartorius muscles of his upper legs. He was frustrated, angry and powerless, sick at the slaughter of innocent people. José had little knowledge of the land across the ocean; New York, Washington and Chicago were places on a map, but exactly *where* on the map, he had no idea. He'd heard of Lincoln, Kennedy and King, and the Space Programme had seared itself into his imagination; but he'd never met an American, didn't know how they lived, how they thought or what their dreams were, and until now hadn't given it much consideration, none at all.

Today, everything changed. José, in his mind, became a citizen of the world. Remembering that somewhere he'd seen or read that a third of New York's population was Hispanic, he became an American, he became a Spanish American. 'Hispanic,' he said aloud, spitting out the last two syllables, assuring himself that this somehow connected the two countries. 'Same difference,' he informed the agitated anchorman, 'Spanish, Hispanic; same thing.'

José's mind wandered across the waters, taking his legs, body and soul with it. He walked the streets of a beleaguered city, looked into sunken eyes staring from dust covered faces and became a survivor, one in a crowd of perplexed, frightened people, a mixture of nations. And in the noisy midst of turmoil between shattered buildings and broken bodies, and surrounded by firetrucks, secretaries, ambulances, policemen, drifts of paper, businessmen, seas of glass, sirens, explosions and the cries of humanity, José wanted retribution, divine, immediate and devastating; he needed to kick out at the perpetrators of this ungodly act.

María brought him another can of beer, and as she began setting out plates of bread, ham, salami and tomatoes, José wondered at the hatred that could spew forth such a ferocious attack against humanity, against civilians whose only faux pas had been to go about their daily tasks.

'Bastards,' he mumbled into the depths of the beer can.

'Who dear,' María asked, anxious, transferring her glance back and forth between her husband and the television set.

'Whoever,' José seethed.

* * *

And that was it, that was a week ago, one short week in which the world had changed; forever.

The newspaper in José's hands was becoming heavy, and the beer and the warm sunshine seemed to be having the same effect on his eyelids. A bee, hovering above the table, eyed briefly the lake of spilt alcohol, then buzzed away as a fly crash-landed and began sucking the liquid into its trumpet-like mouth.

José's hands fell into his lap, and the paper, suddenly coming to terms with gravity, landed on top of them. José's head moved slowly forward, jowls folding into themselves one after the other as they came to rest against his chest.

3. Beach

The gelid horizon was indistinct, vibrating in simmering heat, and then slowly, gently, the hovering vapours collapsed into the form of a caravanserai, a whole baggage-bedecked family making its way along a dusty track. Every now and then one of them would stumble as his foot chanced to land on one of the many loose stones littered across the path.

José, exuberant and impatient to get to the beach, kept running ahead of the party but wasn't quite brave enough to disappear altogether. Occasionally, lost in his headlong rush, he'd find himself coasting around a bend in the track and, alarmed by sudden isolation, would have to retrace his steps until once again the cavalcade hove into view. And what a cavalcade it was, four generations on the move with members of each age group, individually – Grandma being the exception – and together, carrying something: provisions, tables, chairs, rugs, a bundle of linen, and a baby.

José had been given the important task of being in charge of four long sticks, which his father had cut from a clump of canes they'd come across when parking the cars. At first dismayed at having to make himself useful, Jose quickly took onboard the sense of festival and came to enjoy the feeling of responsibility that seemed somehow to be attached to the wooden poles. Also, he quickly lost his apprehension of the thick scrub lining each side of the track. Here he was, the fearless picador, armed and ready for combat with any type of beast that might decide to wander out of the jungle. Feeling happy and in control of the situation, José scanned between the tall pine trees, and although still at some distance, he could see the sun-speckled sea seemingly beckoning him onwards, urging him to quicken his pace. He turned round and waved the sticks in the air.

'Come on!' he exhorted the straggling members of his family. '¡*Venga venga!*'[7]

Returning to the task of leading the retinue, José swung around, the poles swinging with him until they became entangled in a spiky cactus, and the force of momentum threw him off his feet.

'¡*Venga venga!*' his family chorused as he picked himself up and regained possession of the troublesome sticks. He grinned self-consciously at the assembled multitude before once again assuming the role of leader.

At last the party reached the end of the track and grouped itself uncertainly, while Eusebio marched about looking for a suitable place to encamp.

José, however, could wait no longer, a beach was a beach and one section surely couldn't be too much different from another. He sat down and began digging his toes into the hot sand, flexing them backwards and forwards, revelling at the sensation caused by the tiny abrasive grains rubbing between his toes. Squealing with delight, he smacked the surface of the beach with the palms of his hands and then, bending his legs and raising his knees upwards, dug his heels downwards, applying as much force as he was able. He shuffled his feet deeper and deeper until, buried to the ankles, he became aware that the sand beneath the surface was a lot cooler.

He kicked himself free, rolled onto his belly and repeated the digging process, using his toes as miniature excavation devices; flex, bend, backwards and forwards – ooh, this was fun, this was euphoria, this was everything he'd hoped it would be, and more. He imagined himself as some sort of animal that was trying to hide itself and furiously wriggled his toes deeper into the cool layers of sand. He began to laugh, but soon had to stop as he realized that his intakes of breath were filling his mouth with the gritty substance. He extracted his feet and sat up, spitting gobbets of sand in all directions.

José looked towards the sea and had to squint against the reflective glare of sunshine. With index fingers pressed length-wise against his forehead, thumbs against his temples, he cupped his hands above his eyebrows and surveyed the scene in front of him. Magic, he thought, pure magic.

Vaguely, he remembered being brought to the beach last year and had been certain that the sand was golden, but no, now it appeared to be some sort of dirty brown, tinged with grey. The sea, however, was just as he recalled – blue, bluer than anything he'd ever seen, an extreme blue with depth and sparkle, a colour out-matching that of any sky he remembered seeing. In fact, as he thought about it, José began a comparison between the two, sea and sky, blue and blue. He looked straight ahead at the restless body of water and then looked up at the heavens stretched out above him. 'Hmm,' he reckoned, as the sky paled into insignificance.

Suddenly, there was movement at the periphery of his

vision and a flock of seagulls wheeled out of nowhere, screaming directions to each other as they headed towards a fishing boat just visible against the blurred horizon. He watched as the birds sailed effortlessly through the air, and, in his mind, became one of them. He flapped imaginary wings and slid across the sky, then, pointing his head downwards, swooped towards the sea, levelling out at the last moment to glide insouciantly a hair's breadth from the glassy canopy. José cavorted across the wide expanse of sand, imitating perfectly the random undulations of the feathered fraternity until, wondering how he was going to execute an unrehearsed landing, he threw himself into a series of cartwheels, a blur of arms and legs heading towards the expectant surf. One of his hands encountered something hard and slippery, a stone. Wild demons told him it was a prodigy of the deep, more than likely the eye of some scaly monster which even now was opening its terrible maw, eager to swallow the annoyance that had dared to shove a fist into its cyclopean vision. The terrifying thoughts cascaded through José's mind and threw him off balance, body and limbs splashing into the foam-flecked brine. Surrounded by water, he sat up and gasped for breath, ready to fight the hideous beast that he knew was coming to get him. Shaking his head to clear his face of hair and water, he discovered his legs stretched out in front of him, his knees two knobby islands jutting above the ruffled surface. The boy grinned and began to laugh, while droplets of water, expelled from his hair, turned themselves into brilliant diamonds caught in the rays of the sun.

José wasn't scared, not really. Surprised, yes, but not scared, despite finding himself alone at the edge of this vast slab of water. He thought back to last year, autumn, when the pewter sea had stirred sullenly and dark clouds had sailed across a moody sky, obliterating the sun. Hand-in-hand he and his father had stood at the intermittent water's edge, searching vainly for a grey horizon. He remembered his fear, remembered trying to pull away from Eusebio, his little feet gouging tracks of desperation into the treacherous surface of uncaring sand.

Although it was part of his everyday life, José had never been so close to this sleeping vastness, had never imagined how it connected to the edge of the world, the safety of solid earth and the sanctity of trees, houses and mountains. Every day he'd seen it in the distance, motionless and forbidding, and every day he'd wondered. Occasionally, a ship would scratch its way across the blue surface and José would gaze in awe, and in the evenings he'd stare spellbound at shimmering golden reflections as the burning sun spiralled to a watery death underneath Gibraltar. Viewed from the secure isolation of the *cortijo*, the Mediterranean, serene and majestic in its immensity, had never given José cause for alarm until he'd stood here, right *here*, last year with his father.

And now he was part of it, sitting on the edge of infinity, surrounded by a magical entity that had tendrils reaching into every port. He raised his hands and then brought them down to smack hard against the water. Here I am, he thought, me, alone in the sea.

Alone? He looked around. Where *was* everybody?

He surveyed one-hundred-and-eighty degrees of gently moving water; *nada*,[8] his body and knees were the only objects visible above the blue serendipity. Placing his palms onto the sand behind him, he looked upward, eyes narrowing as his gaze pierced the firmament, parallel lines of vision escaping the bounds of earth to speed away beyond the planets.

'José!' his father called from another universe.

José pushed his hands through wet hair and stood up, his nakedness bronze in the midday sun. He turned and sploshed slowly towards terra firma.

'José,' his mother admonished. 'I thought I told you not to go near the sea?'

The boy removed his head from the towel which had been thrown at him by his brother, Jaime. 'It's where I landed,' he replied, shrugging off the easy explanation.

'Don't be stupid,' his father remonstrated.

'I'm not, I did. I really did.'

'You . . . landed?'

'Yup.' José was adamant.

'From where?' Eusebio was equally adamant.

'The sky,' José answered, shaking his head at the stupidity of elders.

'The sky?' his mother asked.

'Yes, the sky, of *cour*se the sky. I was a bird and I fell out of the *sky.*'

'It's the sun,' José's brother said, helping himself to a wedge of bread and a chunk of greasy salami. 'Finally, it's got to him.'

'No, it's true,' José insisted. 'I was a seagull and I didn't know how to land so I crashed into the sea.'

Happy to have enlightened his family, he edged towards the small collapsible table and took some bread and a piece of stale-looking cheese, which, having been encased for too long in a scrap of greaseproof paper, had started to sweat.

The shelter was of simple construction: four long sturdy canes, José's precious canes, stabbed into the sand, each forming the corner of a square with sides measuring roughly two metres, and an old sheet, tied at the corners with odd pieces of string and fastened haphazardly to the supports. The edifice was ungainly, unsightly, and had there been the slightest of breezes the whole contraption certainly would have collapsed. But the day was calm, the sun was high, and the flimsy canopy offered a protective rectangle of shade, which was being taken advantage of not only by the picnic, but also by Conchita, José's grandmother.

Conchita loved these outings to the beach. She loved any outing, anywhere; anything in fact that got her out of the house. On the appointed day she'd be standing just inside the doorway, immobile, like a parcel waiting to be collected, and always she'd be wearing the same clothes, clothes she wore day in, day out, black – the prerequisite colour for a widow. She'd be standing impatiently, smelling of soap, a lace shawl thrown over her shoulders, and she'd be leaning on her cane, bony hands clasped tightly over the intricately detailed pewter knob. At her feet would be the large brown leather bag which everyone knew contained a bottle of home-made wine, a small paper bag full of peppermints, a book, and two small wooden boards upon which she'd sit, because she found the collapsible chairs that were used for the beach, quite unbearable. Jaime, being older than José, was given the onerous task of carrying and being responsible for the holdall, and on several occasions was heard to complain about 'being followed by grandma's beady eyes everywhere I go'.

José sat on the sand and nibbled at the cheese. He looked over his shoulder towards his grandmother, saw her tired old body slumped over the contours of the deck chair and realized that she was fast asleep.

Conchita was the oldest person José had ever seen, older even than the priest, who one day had frightened him almost out of his skin. The youngster had been walking home from school, hands in pockets, feet scuffling at the dust and pebbles of the unmade road. He'd just reached the point at which the homeward track sloped away uphill, when he came became aware of someone standing in front of him. Having been staring fixedly at the track, looking for columns of ants, José suddenly found himself staring at Father Ignacio's high-cut black leather boots.

José stopped, as though brought to a halt by a brick wall. He drew his hands out of his pockets before realizing that he didn't know what to do with them, so, as if hanging them out to dry, he held them up, stretched out sideways in supplication. His gaze tracked upwards from the Father's boots, taking in the black trouser-legs, the black shirt burdened with a white back-to-front collar, the black cloak falling in long elegant folds from the shoulders, and the black hat perched on the priest's head.

Mesmerized by the spectacle in front of him, and far from experiencing feelings of a saintly, religious nature, José deemed the inky apparition to be something that must have been conjured up out of evil. He looked to the right, at an olive tree and a small whitewashed shelter with its iron gate protecting a deep well, and wondered if this strange person had somehow climbed out of the depths and through the metal grille. But no, it wasn't possible – the clothes were dry; and anyway, there was no way this tall man could have squeezed through the narrow gaps between the bars.

'José,' a deep voice boomed out. 'José.' There it was again.

Trying to envisage where the voice had come from, José peered into the dark and deeply lined face. It was useless. On account of the deep shadow hanging under the broad rim of the priest's hat, it was almost impossible to discern any features, let alone a mouth, an orifice for speech, on the sun-tanned face.

'How . . ?'

'How do I know your name?' the man asked.

'How, how do you kn-know my name?' José stammered in agreement, vehemently nodding his head.

'I know everybody's name,' the man replied.

'Where . . ?'

'Where did I come from?' the priest cut in, pre-empting yet again.

'Where did you come from?' José asked, feeling a little bolder.

'Everywhere, José,' the priest answered. 'I come from everywhere. I bring the word of God and the love of Jesus.'

'How?' José was amazed, if not a little sceptical.

The priest laughed; loud, deep and resonant. 'How?'

'Yes,' José agreed, placing his little hands on his hips. 'How?'

'Child,' the holy man said. 'It is not for us to ask about the ways of the Lord. We, all of us, have merely to acknowledge his universal power and accept his gracious love.'

'How?' José was adamant. José wanted to know. Mysteries were no good to him, he needed details; everything had to be spelled out, i's dotted, t's crossed.

'You don't come to Sunday school, José, do you?'

'No,' José replied. 'My brother takes me but loses me on the way.'

'Maybe you lose him?' the priest suggested.

'Well . . .' José faltered, 'it's kind of an arrangement.'

José heard the clicking of bones as the elderly man leaned forwards.

'How so?'

'The arrangement?' José asked, looking up into the dusky face.

'The arrangement,' the priest confirmed.

'Well, my brother . . .'

'Jaime,' the priest stated.

'Yes, Jaime,' José agreed, slowly, suspiciously. 'Well, he says it saves time.'

'What saves time?'

'Me, going to collect last week's paper from Grandma,' José explained.

'And what do *you* get out of this . . . arrangement?'

'Lemonade.'

'I see, lemonade. Well, José, it seems you boys have got it all worked out.'

José thought he saw movement on the old man's face, a fold of skin, a wrinkle; something had crawled across infinite darkness and José was certain the priest had winked at him.

He was told to rest. This was customary and happened every day, excursion or no excursion, special day or festival; after lunch José was supposed to lie down for half-an-hour or so. Whether or not he actually went to sleep was not the point, it was just that José's mother, like all mothers and like most institutions, thought it important that the body should be given a rest after the midday meal. He stomped off and sat down heavily on the cool sand in the shade of the fluttering shelter, next to his grandmother whose large frame was supported on the two wooden boards that had been positioned precariously across the frayed canvas of the deck chair. Conchita looked down at her grandson and searched in her leather bag.

'José,' she commanded. 'Have a mint.'

He took the proffered sweet, popped it into his mouth and sucked morosely as he lay on his side and watched an army of sand flies going about their business. He was restless and soon became bored with the antics of busy little creatures. Sitting upright, he drew his legs towards him, bending them at the knees and capturing them by slinging his arms around them. Lowering his chin onto this pyramid-shaped support of tangled limbs, José scowled at the shoreline and an attendant family of gulls standing with their feet in the ebb and flow of marginal surf.

His grandmother started to snore as a result of having a full belly, though perhaps more as a result of consuming too much home-made wine. Whichever, nodding off was something she did frequently; she didn't care where she did it and she didn't care who knew. José listened to the air rattling in the old woman's throat and, in a mood of quiet contemplation, found the murmur comforting and quite soporific. He closed his eyes and drifted.

Conchita became profoundly uncomfortable. Shifting about on her boards, she tried transferring her weight from one numb cheek to the other, and in the process, farted.

José woke up and shivered, he'd been dozing in the shade for too long. He looked about and saw his brother at the water's edge, doing some strange sort of dance routine, which seemed to involve describing a circle and throwing an occasional spadeful of sand into the air. José became instantly alert and, at five years of age, his young muscles elevated him quickly into action. He stood up and looked down at his grandmother who'd hitched herself into a less uncomfortable contortion, and then he noticed that his parents also had succumbed to after-lunch lethargy and drowsiness caused by the vapid afternoon heat. Creeping out of slumbering shadows, he returned to the world of the living and raced towards Jaime, careening into him and sending him flying.

'*¡Eh, coño!*[9] Jaime screamed at his younger brother. '*¿Qué pasa?*[10]

Giggling with delight, José ran around in tight circles while Jaime pulled himself to his feet. The older boy, quite evidently, had recently been into the water – his woollen bathing trunks, caked in wet sand, were hanging baggily down to his knees – and, as if conscious of the clown-like spectacle, used both hands to drag the sodden material upwards into a more respectable position around his hips.

José began to feel giddy and came to a dizzy halt beside his brother, and together the two lads looked at the excavations that Jaime had been digging. Circular in shape and with a diameter of about one-and-a-half metres, the centre was piled high with sand removed from the trench. Without saying a word, the brothers seemed to know what to do, and while Jaime worked away at shovelling sand, José wandered about collecting stones and pebbles to place on top of the ever-growing mound. They whistled while they went about their tasks, random tunes picked out of the ozone with a chorus provided by the sound of the sea and the cries of wheeling gulls.

Later, Eusebio came to investigate and stood watching as the moat slowly filled with water, some seeping up and out of the sand and some, in the form of gentle waves, trickling over the lip every time the sea lapped far enough up the beach. He turned and walked away, but a few minutes later, returned with a sun-bleached stick and four or five black and white feathers. Jumping across the half-full moat, he shoved the stick firmly into the centre of the sandcastle and placed the feathers at regular intervals around the crown, proud standards laying claim to this small section of the Spanish Empire.

Conchita woke up and began issuing orders from her throne beneath the makeshift awning.

'Inmaculada, what's the matter with you? Where's the bag to put all the rubbish in? Where's Eusebio and those two lads of his? Why aren't they helping?' She rummaged in her leather bag, then, calamity. 'Who's stolen my mints?'

A couple of anxious minutes passed, then, 'No no, it's okay. Found them.' The elusive sweets, having been spilled from the up-ended paper bag, had been located lying about in individual bliss in the depths of Conchita's carryall. However, it wasn't over, the storm had yet to subside. 'Has anyone seen my book? It was here before lunch and now it's gone. And where's my blanket? I might need that later, you know, when it gets cooler?'

Pandemonium. Whenever Conchita went into one of her "moments", there was always pandemonium. Nobody really knew what caused these monumental outbursts, Conchita least of all, but she was the Big Mama, the matriarch, and as such was held in awe and respect by everyone.

Drawn by the sound of commotion, José and Jaime warily approached the rectangle of shadow beneath the gently rippling protective sheet.

'At last! Come on boys, jump to it.'

Conchita sat, hugely proud and hugely in charge of protocol. With fluttering arms and flashing eyes, she directed Jaime to stand on tiptoe and work around the perimeter of the shelter, undoing the cords that held the whole contraption together. Young José's task was to collect the pieces of string as they fell to the ground.

They were too quick, too efficient at their allotted duty; the sky fell in and the head honcho disappeared from view beneath the dirty brown-grey sheet.

'Get it off me, get it off me,' she shrieked. 'What *are* you doing? Why are you so *stu*pid? Why don't you listen?'

The family grouped itself around the heap of flailing material and, despite their laughter, tried to rescue Conchita from her self-induced indignity.

The restaurant was bright, brash and noisy, and boasted the best seafood in town. Nine o'clock and the place was heaving. Waiters, like drones in pre-ordained, drug-enhanced orbit, were scuttling hither and thither, ferrying fish from kitchen to table and returning with empty dishes and leftovers gathered from satisfied, satiated customers. Hugging the promenade, the establishment was a family favourite and the manager, seeing Eusebio and Inmaculada leading the troops into his domain, immediately began to fuss about, shoving three square tables together and repositioning a clutch of chairs so as to give adequate seating around the newly-formed rectangle. José's grandmother sat herself at one end and José was placed at the other, his mother to his left, his father on the right. The rest of the family slotted themselves in where they could.

Stupefied by the unremitting light provided by too many neon tubes and assailed by the potent level of babble, José looked around in amazement. Everybody was talking at once, backwards and forwards, the dialogue augmented by wild gesticulation. It was like a battle, Babel incarnate, words and sentences being pitched across the carnage of dishevelled salads and decimated fish at a volume approaching full throttle. The vocal orchestrations were further enlivened by shouted orders, '*Dame cuatro cañas, cuatro ponches y un agua, cuatro de pez espada, un lenguado, una rosada a la plancha, dos gambas pil-pil y cuatro platitos de patatas fritas.*'[11]

In addition, frequent altercations broke out between the customers, noisy ones, seated at tables that didn't necessarily have to be adjacent to one another but, more often than not, were located at opposite ends of the restaurant.

'*¡Eh, Pablo! ¿Qué pasa?*' Statements, short and sharp, sailed above the diners.

'*¿Y tú, qué tal?*'[12] Questions, responses and general conversation shot back and forth.

It was one giant extended family gathering and José, wincing as the noise level increased in direct proportion to the amount of alcohol consumed, sat in his own little world at the end of the table and tried to fathom it all out. He looked at the expanse of table in front of him and at the two rows of adults, mouths moving in loosened complexity, and then his eyes devoured the complimentary dishes of olives and pimientos and the plates of freshly cut bread. He reached out and helped himself to one of the pimientos.

'José!' The booming voice rolled the length of the tables and caused heads to turn. Conchita had spoken, and everyone waited with baited breath to see what would follow.

'José, don't eat that,' came the command. Conchita had the eyes of a hawk.

'But . . .'

'Don't eat it, José,' Conchita repeated her warning. 'It'll burn your mouth and make your eyes fall out.'

Fortunately for José, his grandmother had deduced that the pimientos were of the dangerously fiery variety, known as *pimientos de Padrón*,[13] thereby saving him from the possibility of searing discomfort.

Along with sharp eyesight, Conchita had been gifted with another formidable weapon in the shape of the two-edged sword which she carried in her mouth at all times. Conchita's tongue could be divisive, decisive and deadly, and was feared widely.

Having finished with the protection of young José, Conchita turned her attention to his mother. 'Inmaculada, what sort of mother do you think you are? How could you not have seen what the boy was about to do? *Good*ness *gra*cious girl, you're sitting right there, right *next* to him.'

'That'll do, mother,' Eusebio hissed at the old lady. 'The danger is over.'

'Don't you take sides, my boy,' Conchita fumed. 'Not against your mother, not when you know she's right.'

Face flushed, Inmaculada acquiesced. 'It's alright,' she said, 'the moment has passed. I'll keep a closer watch over him from now on.'

'The moment need not have occurred in the first place,' Conchita responded haughtily, underlining the word "moment", taunting, pushing at the boundaries. 'To let a child eat one of those things; honestly, I just don't know.'

'Grandma,' Jaime's young voice chirruped. 'He didn't eat it. You saved him! You stopped his eyes from falling out.'

Everyone looked at José in order to establish the veracity of Jaime's statement. José blinked rapidly, trying to hide the fact that his eyes were watering with embarrassment.

Conchita squirmed uncomfortably in her seat. 'Yes, well, perhaps I did,' she acknowledged.

José desperately wanted the floor to open up and swallow him whole, in the same manner as the perceived monster of the depths. What a day! First, he'd made a fool of himself by tripping over his precious bundle of canes; '¡Venga, venga!' everyone had yelled at him. Then, late in the morning, he'd gone against his mother's wishes and ventured into the sea, making himself out to be stupid by pretending to be a seagull. And now, here in the restaurant, he was in trouble yet again, while his grandmother, heavily occupied in doing what she did best, used her wicked tongue to split the family into factions.

'Every year it's the same,' Eusebio pointed out, looking up to meet the simmering gaze of his mother. 'We bring you to the beach and there you sit, in the shady splendour of your own personal tent, fomenting like some unstable volcano, then, after drinking too much, you start to vent your spleen upon your nearest and dearest.'

'It's all right, Eusebio,' Inmaculada said, trying to calm the situation.

'No. Let him have his say,' Conchita commanded, equal to the accusation, formidable in stature as head of the family, safe in the knowledge that everyone would bow to her superiority.

'Well, all I'm saying is . . . is that next year you might find yourself standing imperiously on your doorstep all day long, waiting and wondering,' Eusebio blurted out, knowing that sooner or later, horns would clash.

Conchita puffed herself out, rather in the manner of a disgruntled hen, black clothes rippling dangerously, more threatening than bubbling magma. Just as she opened her mouth to speak, two waiters arrived in the nick of time and promptly set about the distribution of food.

The diners lifted their knives and forks and from the instant of the first plate being placed on the table, the thunderous silence was shattered by the noise of utensils on china.

José picked up a chip and placed it into his mouth, relishing the taste of the greasy potato. He moved it around his mouth and chewed thoughtfully, eyeing his grandmother who seemed to have diminished in size, her ruffled feathers having subsided with the timely arrival of food. He felt something poking him, to the left, *there*, just below his ribs. He caught the movement of his mother's hand as it returned to its task of holding her knife. He looked up at her face.

'There will be consequences,' she whispered, conspiratorially. 'Consequences, José.'

José swallowed his chip, unsure of his mother's meaning.

It was late, later, José thought, than ever before. Bedtime was normally eight or half-past-eight, never later than nine; but they hadn't got home until after ten-thirty. The meal had gone on and on, and with more drinks and with more food, the conversation had started up again, gradually reverting to its original high-pitched fervour.

Conchita, after nearly choking on a fish-bone, had had to be helped to the lavatory, and upon returning to the table had promptly forgotten the direction of her argument and fallen asleep. The long laborious return from the coast involved a frustrating drive through Vélez, one car following the other at snail's pace, while the inebriated occupants tried to remember the location of aunt Esther's house. At last they found it, but because the street was so narrow, eventually diminishing into a track no wider than a footpath, both drivers found themselves having to reverse quite some distance. Thirty minutes later, Conchita decided she needed to pee.

'But, we're nearly home,' Eusebio told her. 'Five minutes, no more.'

'I need to go. Now.' Conchita was obdurate. 'Stop the car!' she yelled.

The car was stopped and Conchita was helped to the side of the road, where, supported on either side, she was lowered into a squatting position above the dark dusty track.

José shifted onto his side and thought about consequences and who would have to face them. Because of all the trouble he'd caused, he thought maybe it would be him, but then he supposed it could be his father who'd be catching these consequences – it was a dangerous occupation, picking a verbal fight with grandma Conchita. Then again, he reasoned, maybe it would be Conchita herself who'd be copping it; after all, she'd been the one who'd started the argumentation.

An owl hooted nearby, its strident call cutting through the background threnody of chattering cicadas and crashing deep into José's thoughts. He opened his eyes and regarded the distant moon, a large pale-yellow face that filled the tiny window. He moved onto his back, linked his hands behind his head and contemplated life. Would it always be so difficult and so confusing, he wondered, or as time marched onwards, would it become any easier?

4. Mid-morning

'José!' the voice called out. 'José!'

José had had enough and tried to retreat further into his shell. Christ! he thought, what have I done now?

'José!'

The restaurant disappeared and bright sunlight danced across his eyelids.

'What did I do?' he asked petulantly, instinctively reaching out as he felt something slither across his arms. His fingers came into contact with the moving object and he tried to latch onto it, managing to grasp one of the pages before the rest of the newspaper fell to the floor.

'It's what you didn't do,' a voice came from above.

He opened his eyes and saw the Madonna gazing down at him, bright sunshine forming a golden halo around her head.

'I thought you had things to do today?' the Madonna enquired, smiling at him.

'Eh?' José grunted.

'You know, things?' María said, holding out her hands Madonna like, as though indicating exactly what she meant.

'Things?' José asked.

'Or maybe not,' María chuckled. She turned and picked up a bowl of potatoes from the table. 'Well, here's something for you to do,' she said. 'Peel these.'

'You're back from the village, then?' José observed, pulling himself upright in his armchair, taking the bowl from his wife and settling it onto his lap. 'Knife?' he asked.

María handed him the implement and he picked up the nearest potato, turning it over in his left hand, deciding where to make the first incision.

María disappeared into the house and turned on the tap. 'José,' she called.

'Can't hear,' he yelled back. Bloody woman, he thought, always talking to me from a distance.

'What?' María shrieked.

José concentrated on peeling potatoes. He heard the tap being turned off, followed by the sound of advancing footsteps as María pattered outside.

'What's the matter with you?' she shouted at him.

'You're here now,' he told her, 'no need to shout. What do you want?'

'If you've got no plans for the afternoon, you might like to help me with the white-washing,' María suggested.

'Mmm,' José replied.

'I made a good start this morning, nearly half done already.'

'So that's the secret,' José remarked. 'That's why you get up at the crack of dawn.'

'With you out of the way I can get things done,' María told him. 'Besides, it's nice and cool first thing.'

'Mmm,' José muttered, scratching the side of his nose with the point of the knife. 'How long 'til lunch?'

'Lunch!' María exclaimed. 'It's not midday yet and you're thinking of lunch?'

'Get me a beer, then,' José ordered, 'and something to eat. I'm starving.'

María walked back into the kitchen, tut-tutting as her flip-flops flapped against the tiles. José smiled to himself and returned to the task of relieving the potatoes of their skins.

A few minutes later, María reappeared with a tray of food. She plonked it on the table and then returned to the kitchen for José's beer and a cup of coffee for herself. Sitting on the little wall bordering the patio, she watched her husband stab a slice of tomato and place it on a chunk of bread. Onto the tomato went a slice of thick fatty salami and a wedge of hard oily cheese, and then the whole ensemble was lifted through the air to José's mouth. As his teeth bit into the unstable pile of food, he winked at María, happy to be eating, happy with life in general.

Alerted by the familiar sound of his son's ancient Land Rover, José looked across the valley and saw the telltale plumes of dust raised by the long-base wagon as it growled along the parched track. There had been no rain since March and the countryside was tinder dry. The normal autumn rainfall had not materialized, and apart from a couple of storms last year in late November, there had been nothing, not a drop. The lakes were at their lowest levels since about forty years ago and the outlook was bleak.

José glanced towards the drying beds sloping away below the *cortijo*. He gazed at the serried ranks of grapes, clump after burnished clump lying under the relentless sun. Every day María would hunker down onto the soil between the rows of fruit and turn the bunches over, arranging them neatly, and every day the grapes would shrink a little smaller until, after five or six weeks, the succulent berries became raisins. It was a labour of love, one that annually produced less and less financial reward, the industry being undermined by cheap imports from the fertile valleys of California.

The locals preferred to put their crops to another use, that of wine production, a process as old as the surrounding hills. The harvested muscat grapes were placed in vats into which a wooden disc was lowered and slowly, laboriously, screwed down, pressing out the vital juice. The resultant brew, land-wine – sweet, heady and strong – was stored in large wooden casks from which the farmers took their daily supplies in an assortment of plastic bottles and containers.

The thrumming of the Land Rover faded as the vehicle disappeared behind the hummocks at the head of the valley, and then, reappearing, the deep-throated roar of the engine and the noisy crunching of gears began to intensify as the car lumbered along on its approach to the homestead.

José tapped his stick impatiently against the terracotta floor of the patio as he watched his son climb out of the vehicle. '*Buenos*,'[14] he said, smiling at the swarthy dark-haired man striding towards him.

Vicente sat on one of the plastic chairs and grinned lop-sidedly at his mother as she placed a can of beer onto the table beside him. He nodded appreciatively and removed his straw hat, placing it on another of the plastic chairs. He flipped the tab and opened the can, taking a long draught of the cold liquid before leaning forward to press the button on the front of the television and sitting back to watch the screen flare into action.

It had become a daily occurrence, father and son sitting in the shade of the patio, absorbing greedily the details that emerged from the ancient purveyor of news. From day one, José had his suspicions, had gone through his list of possible suspects. ETA, the IRA, and that German bunch of fringe lunatics, Baader Meinhof or the Red Brigade or whatever they called themselves, were among those prominent in his daily ruminations. He'd quickly ruled out the Irish stream of terrorism, it received too much finance from its American brotherhood and, supposing it able actually to locate New York, would end up murdering its own descendants, effectively stemming the flow of money and guns.

Transferring his deliberations to the German fraternity, José realized that of late, it had been pretty quiet. 'Hah,' he muttered through an awkward mouthful of long-stalked oversized capers, 'their last outrage was in seventy-two at the Munich Olympics and since then, Mossad has done the job of wrapping them up and closing them down.' He turned his mind to ETA, the group that sometimes was linked to the IRA and, by association, also linked to America. No, he decided, it wouldn't be the Basques, they were too territorial, preferring to restrict their activities to the Iberian Peninsula.

Through a slow masterful process of elimination, José shortened the list and ended up reckoning that the only people capable of such crass stupidity would be those 'sand-dwellers', as he called them.

'Sand-dwellers?' Vicente had asked his father.

'Yep, those who consider life incomplete without a tea towel flapping round their ears. Shit, they're so unstable they can't stop fighting amongst themselves, have been for hundreds of years. They don't need wars with anybody else, for Christ's sake, they've got their own private never-ending battle.'

'Who?' Vicente asked. 'Arabs?'

'A select few,' José had explained. 'A few misguided fanatics.' He chuckled, a sort of primaeval grunt, as he remembered the civil war and the great divide that had churned his own country into a smouldering cauldron of hate.

José had been right in his assumptions. In the space of one long day it had emerged that a group of sabre rattling Muslims, vowing to rid the earth of infidels, had shouted *"Jihad"*. And the world had been insulted.

And now there was a strange feeling that permeated everything, everywhere. It was as though for a few days, time had stood still; a handful of hours during which the planet breathed in and breathed out, and waited with expectation and trepidation; the world was aghast and wanted answers. Who were these people who'd come hurtling out of a lazy blue September sky? And why?

And then a name came sliding out of the crackling speaker; Osama Bin Laden, the man who claimed responsibility, the man who had slammed his disciples of suicide into buildings that housed no military installations, towers that in no way resembled barracks stuffed full of armed gladiators; these were soft targets, offices inhabited by mothers, fathers, sons and daughters. America would retaliate, had to retaliate; eye for eye, tooth for tooth – biblical terms, the only language these bead-counting terrorists would understand. Ambivalence found no harbour in José's reasoning, a rationale sharpened after the horrors of Guernica, and he would gladly do battle with the men who'd planned this atrocity; these were not people with whom to parley over glasses of sugared mint tea.

But nothing happened.

The world breathed in, the world breathed out, gently, quietly, and civilization paused on the edge of credulity. The West showed restraint as it counted its dead, and day by day while the dust settled on Manhattan, the dawn of realization unfolded. War had been declared on democracy.

The two men watched the flickering screen, occasionally shaking their heads in disbelief as the footage was re-run; carnage on a grand scale, bravery, confusion, destruction, and the indelible mark of Muhammad.

'They're saying there's going to be a war,' Vicente told his father.

'They? Who?'

'The villagers.'

José looked up as María emerged from the sanctuary of the kitchen. He watched while she fussed about with yet another plate of food, trying to find some space on the already crowded tabletop, and noticed the worry on her face. Then, looking at his son, he relaxed, feeling safe and secure with his family around him, forgetting for a moment the crisis that gripped the world.

He leaned forward, hands resting on the top of his cane. 'They're right,' he said. 'Except . . . except it's already started. It started when the first aircraft flew into that tower.' He pushed a plate of food across the table. 'Go on,' he said, helping himself to another chunk of salami. 'Eat something.'

'No, I've got work to do,' his son replied, getting to his feet. 'That water tank I've been building. Need to get the cover finished before too much dust gets inside. I've got the beams in the back of the Landrover and Pepe's supposed to be coming to help me get them on top of the tank.'

'It's all gone to shit,' José said.

'What has?' Vicente asked.

'The world, and everything in it,' his father told him. 'Mark my words, the world is a different place.'

Vicente picked up his hat and shoved it on his head, dark brown eyes peering out from under the brim. He wandered towards the Landrover. 'Maybe,' he acknowledged, then, over his shoulder, 'Back for lunch.' He swung himself into the seat, switched the ignition and slammed the door, grinning as the ancient vehicle lurched into life. He reversed up the slope and onto the track, changed gear and headed back the way he had come, deep-treaded tyres gouging dust and flinging it into the air. He thought he heard a voice and looked into the broken, duck-taped wing mirror to see his mother step from behind the cottage and wave her arms.

'Three o'clock,' María yelled at the vehicle as it gathered speed. 'Three o'clock.'

José settled back into his armchair. 'Stupid woman,' he muttered. 'Always yelling and screaming from a distance.' He smiled at María as she returned round the corner of the *cortijo* and asked her to bring him another beer. He didn't bother to finish the old can, it was getting warm, and when María handed him a cold fresh one, he quickly pulled the ring, listening happily to the metallic sound of tearing aluminium. Christ, he thought, it's been a long day. And while his wife busied herself clearing away plates of food and discarded beer cans, he opened the newspaper and tried to concentrate on the columns of print.

Compared to the events currently unfolding on the other side of the world, the paper offered little of interest. He read about a huge fire in a national park somewhere in the mountains near Ronda; far enough away, José thought, they might as well be writing about the moon. He sucked some beer from the can and flicked through a few more pages. Nothing, nothing, nothing. He looked up and noticed the television still playing those images of death and destruction, over and over. On it went, on and on, and as more information came to hand it seemed that the world was emerging from its state of pandemonium and slowly coming to terms with the new régime. Resolutions were being forged. Democracy and freedom opened their eyes, and the western infidels, in taking stock of the situation, determined to stand strong and stand united against the fury of global terrorism. Panic buying had broken out nearly everywhere and airlines, all of them, had been banned from flying in or out of the USA.

So, *that's* what's different about today, José found himself thinking, subconsciously realizing that he could hear the whine of an aircraft dragging its shock-wave over the mountains on its approach to Málaga. He left his chair, stepped off the terrace and walked a few paces to stand in the open space near the garage. He bent his head backwards and gazed at the sky to verify the fact that it *was* an airliner.

While the ban on flying had not been extended to include European airspace, there certainly had been a massive reduction in the amount of short haul flights, but now, aviation seemed to be returning to some sort of normality. José recalled standing in the same place last week and doing the very same thing, searching the heavens for movement. The azure sky had been empty; no clouds, no contrails. And then he'd seen something, something moving quickly, very quickly. It was black and sleek, a dark object which José thought was a jet, a military machine, and then it had turned and dived and opened its wings and José had gazed in admiration as the eagle, searching for any movement on the ground far beneath, described a giant circle against the deep blue background.

He returned to his chair, picked up the paper and found his mind wandering to Pearl Harbour, the surprise attack that turned out to be the biggest mistake Japan ever made, and wondered if this would turn out to be the same sort of epic blunder. He wondered if Uncle Sam was going to take the battle back to the terrorists, back to the zealots and the régime that championed their cause; if so, the crumbling crucible of civilization was in for a serious pounding.

María came struggling out of the shadows, a large tub of paint clutched in both hands.

'Now what are you up to?' José asked her. 'Christ woman, can't you sit still for two minutes?'

'Preparation, José,' she answered. 'Preparation.'

'What about lunch?'

'That'll be next,' María said, depositing the heavy tub onto the floor. She turned, hands on hips, glared at her husband and disappeared back into the cottage. Two minutes later, she reappeared with a long-handled roller and a pair of vivid pink rubber gloves. 'I told you,' she continued, 'this afternoon I'll be painting. Maybe you can mix the paint?' she asked hopefully.

'Hmm,' José grunted as he turned the pages of his newspaper. 'We'll see.'

Vaguely aware of María clattering about in the little kitchen, he closed his eyes against the glare of the sunshine and brought his arms, and the newspaper, to rest on the arms of the chair. He settled back and breathed in, long and deep, slow and luxurious, sensing the atmosphere, the dryness of the air and the hot earth baking beneath the midday sun. Crushed beneath the weighty fragrance of honeysuckle, José relaxed into torpid surroundings.

5. *Feria*[15]

José looked out of the window, nose pressed hard against the vibrating glass.

He was excited and couldn't wait to get off the bus. He brought his face away from the window and looked up and down the length of the quivering vehicle. It seemed as though the other kids were equally excited, most had their attention tuned to the hustle and bustle fomenting across the pavements, across the streets. The mums and dads appeared also to be caught up in the tantalizing *frisson* of adventure.

The bus hummed itself to a halt, shuddering while pistons stopped firing and brakes were applied. It could go no further, its front bumper on kissing terms with a confusion of *char-à-bancs* parked immediately ahead.

The family had roused in the early hours, before the first glimmer of light began to peep through the windows of the *cortijo*. Caught up in the atmosphere of expectation that permeated the little cottage, José had been restive from the word go. He tried to remember if ever before he'd been up and about so early; he didn't think he had.

The morning stretched out ahead, interminable hours and circular minutes, José growing ever more impatient as he rushed about performing his tasks for the day. It was his job, before breakfast, to feed the partridges his father kept in cages fixed to the wall above the patio. Each bird had the privilege of having its own cell, although the prison was not a great deal larger than the bird itself. José always felt sorry for these animals, he'd given them names and would talk with them as he threw a handful of corn mixed with seed into each cage.

Far from being just tuneful ornaments, these birds served a purpose about which José was none too sure. Come the shooting season, father would select the partridges which sang longest and loudest and transport them in their cages into the depths of the *campo*,[16] where they'd sing to their heart's content. Wild partridges, upon hearing the sweet voices of their brethren, were drawn to the area and promptly shot, felled mid-flight by a hail of deadly lead pellets. Of course, José never aired his opinions on this matter for fear of incurring his father's wrath, or worse, ridicule. This savage trickery was the way of life, or rather, death; an established art form, acceptable to those who dwelled in the countryside and handed down from generation to generation, man and bird alike. Whether or not it was acceptable to the bird was not a matter for consideration.

Having fed the birds, José had to make sure that each had sufficient water in the little upside down bottles secured to the side of the cages. The bottles were fitted with rubber teats, which the birds would clamp between their beaks every time they felt the urge; it was surprising how rapidly the water was consumed.

'José, *desayuno*,'[17] his mother called.

He ran round the corner of the *cortijo* and joined his father, who already was seated at the table, studying two bowls of steaming porridge that sat waiting on the embroidered tablecloth. As José sat down, his mother poured the goat's milk. Then came the best part, sugar. José loved sugar, he loved anything sweet, and it was a daily contest to see which of them, father or son, spooned more out of the canister and onto their food. The porridge was followed by bread or *pitufos*[18] drizzled with oil, or spread with jam or honey, or layered with salami or ham or a patina of tomato paste – whatever Inmaculada managed to find in the scullery. While his father drank black coffee and cogitated, José washed down his breakfast with a glass of milk. It was a meal shared between the two men who were sometimes joined at the table by José's older brother, especially in the winter when the countryside became thick with bands of people harvesting nuts and olives. José's mother, having breakfasted a couple of hours beforehand, flustered about them like a mother hen, clearing plates and slicing more bread when necessary.

The work continued after breakfast with a visit to the chickens, feeding them, watering them and collecting their eggs. On rare occasions José would notice that a chicken was missing, taken perhaps by a fox, although the fleet of dogs managed mostly to prevent this happening. At night-time, the dogs – never allowed into the house – were chained up at strategic positions around the chicken runs, and José was often woken by their barking as they yelled discouragement at any creature that dared to move during the starlit hours. Sometimes the dogs would get it into their heads to bark at nothing, and José would lie awake in the middle of night, cursing the stupidity of the four-legged guardians.

Then there was the mule, the pig, and the goats; every day it was José's job to check the ruminants, make sure they had water and give them something to eat. He liked his work, it made him feel important and, at the tender age of seven, he began to realize that he was an integral part of the family, making a contribution to its daily function of survival. Today being a holiday, José's father accompanied him on his rounds, watching as the boy marched to-and-fro carrying buckets of water, replenishing the containers dotted around the farm-stead. He watched as the mule was given some oats and the other animals some dried-up root vegetables. He smiled when he heard José talking to the animals, calling each one by name and stroking its head and, in the case of the pig, smacking it on its broad flanks.

'Papa,' José yelled. 'Look how big this pig has grown. Look, it's twice the size of that goat!'

José was happy, glad to have his father at his side and pleased that his efforts seemed to be satisfactory. Later, with the animals taken care of, the two men, man and boy, walked back to the cottage.

José's clothes had been laid out for him the night before, and now, eagerly, he was pulling on the smart grey shorts which his mother had pressed, sharp creases front and back, and which came to a halt three inches above his kneecaps. He picked up the shirt; it was new, brand new and stripy, green stripes on white. José shoved his arms into the sleeves, long sleeves, and when his hands emerged from the cuffs, his fingers fumbled hastily at the buttons; then he collected the tails together and stuffed them into his shorts, at the same time working his feet into brown leather sandals. He ran out of his room and into his parents' bedroom and finding it empty, continued on into the kitchen. His mother turned from the sink and smiled at him.

'José,' she said, 'come here. You've got your buttons wrong.' She squatted on her haunches and quickly corrected the situation. 'Just like your father,' she told him, standing up and returning to the task of scrubbing potatoes.

José went out to join his father who, cigar in mouth, was sitting on the low wall bordering the patio. They sat and watched as lazy tendrils of thick tobacco smoke hovered in undecided equilibrium before dispersing unhurriedly towards each end of the terrace. After a while, Inmaculada emerged from the kitchen clutching a jug full of lemonade and a plate laden with *empanadillas*, the small pasties stuffed with spiced mince.

At last it was time for them to set forth. They left the house and followed the little path down to the track that led to the village. It took them half-an-hour to reach the plaza, thirty minutes during which the sun blazed down from a cloudless sky, throwing their shadows, short and crisply precise, onto the dusty track behind them.

The bus, decked-out with paper streamers, flags and pennants made of bunting, and multicoloured balloons of various shapes and sizes, looked as though it had been driven straight out of a fairy tale. Noticing that people had already started to board, José and his parents dashed across the plaza and joined the queue curving back towards the street lamp, a mini-roundabout in the centre of the square. Slowly, the line moved forward and the citizens of Arenas took their seats, expectant hubbub growing in stature commensurate with the increasing level of excitement.

Finally, everyone was on board, it was time to go. The driver stepped into the coach, squeezed behind the wheel, and, with decorations flying proudly, the bus pulled away from the plaza.

The forty-five minute journey followed a track which meandered down and around the foothills of the Sierra de Tejeda, every bump and hollow affording José the visual treat of seeing the passengers bounce up and down on the well-worn upholstered seats, a precursor to some of the spectacular rides they would encounter at the fairground. Horn beeping at every opportunity, the bus rumbled through the narrow streets of Vélez-Málaga, pedestrians scrambling to left and right, acceding passage to the benzene-guzzling behemoth of the roads.

Attracting visitors from a wide region around the capital town of the Axarquia, every year the *feria* caused the same problems of congestion. Following a procession of coaches from Competa and Corumbella, Sayalonga and Algarrobo, the driver took his captive audience on a tour of the town's southern quarter, passing the duck-pond and traversing a maze of narrow cobbled-streets before heading towards the centre and the Plaza de las Carmelitas. From here, the Guardia Civil directed the proud, smoke-belching flotilla into a network of neighbouring streets, where, nose to tail, the buses came to a halt and disgorged their human contents.

José looked through the dirty window and was astonished, he'd never seen so many people; swarming around the coaches they were everywhere. Wondering if he should be worried at the size of the crowd, he dragged his eyes from the scene outside and focused on his parents to see if they looked alarmed or perturbed. His father intercepted the glance and smiled, and José's world was filled with reassurance.

The air was vibrant, hot and rancid, full of strange smells invading José's nostrils as he and his parents debarked the bus. The ubiquitous aroma of soap was today intermingled with the bittersweet aroma of sweat. It was July, the temperature was rising, and the masses flowing through the streets of Vélez-Málaga had little or no regard for the excess moisture leaking from their pores. Anxious not to get lost, José gripped firmly his parents' hands as the trio became part of the free-wheeling imbroglio. He soon forgot about the soap and the sweat, there were other, vastly more interesting odours on offer: intriguing aromas of sweet sticky popcorn, sizzling spicy sausages, sizzling fried onions, hot fat, and beer and whisky-breath from bands of swaying male youths, and cloying perfume, sometimes sweet and sometimes musty, from shoals of high-heeled *señoritas.*[19]

It was *feria,* José's first *feria,* and he was out to enjoy himself, but right now he was a little apprehensive. Looking up at his father, and then at his mother, he saw how tall and elegant they were and noticed the manner in which they seemed to glide along the street. Impressed by their appearance, he'd never seen his parents looking so smart.

Eventually, hustled along by seething crowds, they arrived at the Plaza Reyes Católicos, where José, looking ahead through gleaming drops of water thrown into the air by a fountain, caught his first glimpse of the brightly-coloured stalls lining Andalucía Park. He was galvanized into action.

'Mama, papa, look,' he yelled, pulling at their arms as he strained to get closer, wanting to lose himself amongst the dazzling enticements on offer. His parents, laughing, caught up in the spell of José's perceived magic, allowed themselves to be hauled into the fray. The milling crowds swirled and eddied in a majestic dance beneath the polished bottle green leaves of gigantic rubber trees. Standing one moment in front of a stall selling freshly-cut slices of coconut, José and his parents were swept suddenly into the spiralling vortex of the madding multitude and ejected, a few frantic seconds later, next to a kiosk almost buried beneath the printed word. Shelf after sagging shelf of leather-bound tomes, vying for space with paperbacks and periodicals, threatened to buckle the flimsy wooden framework and send it crashing to earth. José feasted his eyes on the rows of books, his imagination boring through the spines, entangling itself virus-wise into the myriad worlds imprisoned amongst the pages. The purveyor of print, noticing the focus of José's vision, selected a battered volume from a collection of second-hand books and presented it to the young lad.

'*Mira, un regalo para tí,*' [20] he said as José held out eager hands.

However, before the youngster managed to make contact with the proffered gift, his father snatched the book out of the vendor's grasp and thrust it back. 'Thank you, but no,' he said, thinking of the pesetas that would have to change hands.

'No no, it's a gift,' said the man with the smile, taking the much-travelled volume and placing it firmly into the boy's out-stretched hands. 'Not enough people read,' he continued by way of explanation. 'You should encourage him.'

With this, he turned and picked up another book, a slim paperback, and dangled it in front of José's saucer-wide eyes.

Grinning sheepishly at his father, José took hold of the slender temptation and pressed it triumphantly against the title already in his hands. Not to be outdone by the display of generosity, Eusebio picked up a copy of the local weekly paper and contributed twice the stated price.

As they stood debating their next move, the swirling sea of humanity unleashed a new wave, a tidal surge that sucked them in and spat them out at another location, another port of call in the midst of the tree-canopied park. The stall, a mountain in miniature of striped candy, buckets of popcorn, blocks of nougat and clouds of pink and white candyfloss, filled their eyes and informed their bellies that breakfast was but a vague memory.

Wandering out of the park, they headed towards the fairground and in a space between the two, found themselves in an area dedicated to the production of cheap greasy food. Tureens of fish soup bubbled alongside kettles of thin, pale-yellow watery stuff, containing pieces of chicken and boiled egg. There were dishes of broad beans mixed with chunks of fried ham; *chorizo*[21] and *salchichón*,[22] raw and fried; tortilla cakes piled high; *boquerones* – filleted raw anchovies drowning in a sea of wine vinegar – and bountiful baskets displaying an infinite variety of bread. Inmaculada had thought to bring a blanket with her, and now she spread it on the dusty ground while Eusebio went to stand in the long queues of hungry revellers.

They sat on their little square of material under the shade of a plane tree, an oasis of tranquillity amidst the hot heaving hurly-burly. Sitting cross-legged, they ate their food and watched the ever-changing permutations as the kaleidoscope flickered and daylight faded to dusk. The world became trans-

formed, incorporating new dimensions as evening slid effortlessly into night, a microcosm strung with coloured bulbs and
fairy lights connecting pillars to posts and trees to buildings,
rainbows of hot electricity daubing lurid colours onto excited
faces.

Later, José and his parents met up with Jaime, and together
as a family they melded into the fantasy. It was while standing at the entrance to the big dipper that José fell in love and
came to understand the meaning of jealousy. Sliding out of
the shadows, a girl, dark of eye, dark of hair, tall and slim and
armed with a smile to fall into, latched herself sinuously to
Jaime's side.

'This is Raquel,' Jaime announced, proudly putting his
arm around the girl's waist.

José's chin became a vexation to his jaw muscles and he
stared open-mouthed at the vision standing before him, the
vision that was being kissed on both cheeks by his parents.
And then the girl was bending down, leaning towards him,
and he felt soft lips land either side of his face. Raquel took
him by the hand and the three youngsters advanced towards
the ride.

The little wooden cars were fitted with two rows of seats
with only enough room for two people on each, but Raquel
and Jaime squeezed José between them, wedging him into
position as the attendant pushed the car along gleaming parallel rails until it hooked itself onto a chain. *Clank, clank,
clank* went the mechanism hoisting the wagon up the steep
slope, and with each inexorable movement of cog, ratchet and
link, José's adrenalin-filled expectations rose towards bursting-
point.

Suddenly they were hurtling earthwards and rows of lights

suspended above the track flashed overhead and disappeared somewhere behind. Faster they went and faster and José blinked rapidly as multicoloured shooting stars came flying out of the black tunnel that was going to swallow them although it was far too small, it was tiny and they were all going to die. José prayed, or thought he did, he couldn't remember because at that precise moment the car zoomed into the circular opening and everyone ducked. There was a sensation of sliding to the left as the rails forced the car into a tight right-hand curve; darkness, darkness, then a pinprick of light expanding into brightness as they shot out of the tube and rejoined the world of the funfair. It seemed as though the car would never make it to the summit of the next gradient, but . . . it did and they were off again and there to the left were José's parents – how did they get there? José wondered – waving madly. Arms pinned to his sides, he could do nothing, so he opened his mouth, felt the wind tearing into him as the car picked up speed, and screamed.

Breathless seconds later, he clapped his hands over his ears to shut out the squeal of protesting brakes as the man pulled a lever and brought the car to a halt. He could feel his body joyously expand back into shape as the trio unpacked themselves and clambered onto the platform, exhilarated and a little unsteady on their feet.

Like a dog on a lead, José trailed his brother and Raquel as they wandered leisurely through the thronging crowds towards the Ferris wheel. He watched them pass through the stile and load themselves onto one of the hanging seats, and when the enormous wheel began to rotate, he moved a little further along the fence until he found a place affording a better view.

Elbows on the railing, he lowered his chin into cupped

hands and gazed at the distant princess as she was transported through the night sky. Up she went, upwards and backwards across the orange face of the rising moon, then down, hair flying out behind her. He could see that she was smiling and, moments later, when she turned her head towards Jaime, watched enviously as his brother pulled her closer. And then the seat passed behind some massive metal supports and José imagined he saw them kissing. Back in view, the couple started again on the upward swing, and José, his vision drilling through space, savoured their passionate embrace. Jealousy coursed through his body and clutched at his entrails; he wanted to be his brother, he wanted to be older, taller; he wanted to touch the soft female skin, breathe the exotic perfume and run his fingers through the sea of shiny, silky black hair; he wanted . . . everything. He stood there, leaning against the fence, transfixed; a small boy lost in a world of noise, lights, and fantasy, disregarding the incessant throng swirling hither and thither. José determined to find a girlfriend for himself, one just as beautiful as the girl swinging through air, and marry her. Time ceased to exist as he plunged his hands into his pockets and discovered the first uncertain pre-pubescent stirrings.

'There you are!' his mother cried, sailing towards him, buoyant on the edge of the crowd. 'Your father's talking to uncle Jorge,' she told him, frowning. 'They're drinking whisky.'

José looked at the ground and smiled. His mother was always annoyed when his father turned to spirits and now she seemed to be having some sort of a panic.

'Is auntie Rosie here as well?' he asked.

'She was, but she's gone home to prepare a room for us.

She's invited us to stay the night, but . . . I don't know. If your father's going to be drinking . . .'

'Oh let's,' José pleaded.

'Well, I don't know,' his mother repeated, undecided.

'Oh please,' José implored. The idea, once implanted, germinated quickly, making him anxious somehow to sway his mother's mind. He knew he'd be able to stay up late if they were guests at his uncle's house; if they didn't have to return to the bus. 'Please mama, please please *please.*'

'Well . . .' Inmaculada looked around as if to find an answer written on the faces of the restless multitudes. 'It does make sense, I suppose,' she said, smiling down at her son. 'Sort of.'

'Yes, mama, of course it does,' he agreed, purring with happiness.

'And . . . tomorrow morning I suppose I could go to the market before we go home.'

'You see, mama, it's a great idea? It's the best.'

Proud to have helped his mother make the correct decision, José stuck out his right hand, placed it into the warm grip of his mother's left hand, and together they went off in search of his father.

* * *

The plate shattered against the wall and a small cloud of minute china particles hovered in an errant ray of early morning sunshine. Frozen in space, the splinters created a spectacular display of coruscating light, fascinating to behold, before falling to the floor, no more than a sigh in the ensuing perfect silence.

It was eight-fifteen and José's parents stood facing each other, a tableau etched in time. Eusebio, back to the wall, was taut with emotion, his neck-muscles raw cords of anger connecting his thrusting jaw with his tense square-shoulders. He couldn't believe, couldn't comprehend the rage and the fury manifesting itself in front of his eyes. Of course, there had been previous occasions when he'd been out drinking – indeed he'd crept home late on several of them – and he knew he was in for a certain amount of trouble and vexation; but this? This was something new, something he hadn't been prepared for. He was totally at a loss and found himself shaking in trepidation of what might come next. Staring across the gulf that separated him from the woman he suddenly didn't know, he saw the fear and the anguish, the pain and hatred in her eyes, noticed the spittle on her lips, and he wondered.

'How could you?' Inmaculada screamed at him. 'How?'

'It was a drink,' Eusebio replied, bringing his arms down to his sides, safe now that the remains of the plate had finished settling onto the floor. 'Just a drink.'

'A drink? A drink? At eight in the morning? What kind of a drink is that?'

'Two or three drinks,' Eusebio admitted. 'I've done it before . . .'

'And that's an ex*cuse*?' Inmaculada raged. 'Never this late, Eusebio, never.' She paused and looked him in the eyes. 'And why last night?' she asked. 'Why did you have to pick last night?' She pointed at him, rigid finger at maximum extension, her whole body trembling with unsuppressed wrath. 'Look at you,' she admonished. 'Just look at the state you're in.'

Eusebio looked down at the slope of his belly, noticed the stains on the shirt, his best shirt, the one he'd worn so proudly when he'd escorted his wife and his son to the *feria*, yesterday, only yesterday. He tried to tuck the shirt-tails back into the waist of his trousers and tried to remember why they'd come out in the first place. His head was beginning to ache and his eyes felt as though someone had been rubbing grains of sand into them. All he wanted to do was lie down somewhere, somewhere dark and peaceful where there'd be no one shouting at him. He needed a drink; no, he didn't, he'd had alcohol enough for a lifetime, but his mouth felt drier than the deserts of Almería and his breath was making him feel nauseous.

'I'm talking to you,' Inmaculada hissed.

'Can't it wait?' Eusebio pleaded. ''Til the morning?'

'It *is* the morning,' he was informed and, after a pause, was asked, 'What sort of example is this? What's José going to think?'

'Where is he?' Eusebio asked, panicking.

'Do you care?' Inmaculada threw at him.

'Jesus!'

'No Jesus,' Inmaculada yelled. 'Where were you last night, you and that useless brother of yours? Did you even stop to *think* about José?'

'Of course.'

'Of course,' Inmaculada snorted. 'You didn't stop to think about anybody. Did you?'

'It was just a drink, Inma, just a stupid drink.'

'How could you, last night of all nights?' She rushed forward, crushed her body against his, pummelled at him with her fists; again and again blows rained down on his unprotected flanks and then she tried to knee him in the groin. Eusebio felt himself going under, the attack had thrown him back against the wall and he started slowly to slide down the smooth surface. Inmaculada reached out, grabbed him by the testicles and pulled with all her might. *That* brought him out of his imagined stupor and he struggled to stand upright, tried to ease the strain that was threatening to tear out his manhood by the roots. He stood on tiptoe and cursed the Lord for not endowing him with longer legs.

'*¡Mierda!*[23] he cried out. 'Let the fuck go.'

Suddenly, the pain in his crotch disappeared and relief, sweet tender relief, swam in to replace the excruciating agony that had clawed at his vitals. The respite was almost as much of a shock to Eusebio's shattered system as the attack on his genitals, and the rapid change of sensation nearly threw him off balance as he sucked in a lungful of air. The peace was short lived. Inmaculada lunged forward with renewed spleen and raked her fingernails down his face, at the same time clamping her teeth vice-like onto his jaw.

There was nowhere for Eusebio to go, he was pinned against the wall. Desperately, clutching at Inmaculada's arms, he managed to drag them to her sides. Forcing them behind her, he used one hand to hold her arms together at the wrists and with the other, removed her mouth from his face. Summoning every ounce of depleted strength, he held her at arm's length, held her while she spat at him and called him an *hijo de puta.*[24]

And then it occurred to him that he had no idea what she was talking about.

'What do you mean you stupid bitch?' he asked. 'What do you mean, "last night of all nights"? What's so special about last night?' He was sweating, panting with exertion, his body trembling with anger and frustration and fear.

'Don't you worry about it,' Inmaculada told him. 'All you have to do is go out and have a good time.'

'What?' Eusebio asked. 'What don't I need to worry about?'

'There's no point anyway, not now.'

Eusebio released his hold on Inmaculada's arms and stumbled to the table. Exhausted, he pulled out a chair and let his body slump into a sitting position. He put his head in his hands and sat, motionless.

Rubbing her wrists, first one and then the other, Inmaculada pulled out one of the other chairs and sat opposite her husband. She placed her hands flat on the surface of the table, moved them back towards her body and let her thumbs trace down over the curved edge. She gripped tightly, pressure causing her knuckles to turn white. 'You never knew, did you?' she asked quietly, a large teardrop rolling down her left cheek.

'What?' Eusebio asked from somewhere in the depths of his large clammy hands. 'What didn't I know?'

'God! You men are *so* ignorant.'

'We are?' Eusebio asked.

'I was *pregnant* for Christ's sake, Eusebio, and all you could do was go out and get drunk.'

'Pregnant?' Eusebio asked, raising his head from the safety of the nest. 'Pregnant? How?'

'*Was*, you stupid fucking ignorant specimen of a man.' Then, softly, she repeated the loathsome word. 'Was.'

Inmaculada started to cry and tried to stifle it. Her body, torn with grief, shuddered silently under the tightly controlled sobs.

'But, but I don't understand,' Eusebio said, slowly getting up from his chair. 'I mean . . .'

'No, of course you don't understand. How could you?' Inmaculada asked.

'But you have to tell me,' Eusebio chided, before correcting himself. 'You *should've* told me.'

'What's there to tell?' she said. 'We had sex, I got pregnant. That's the way it works, Eusebio. That's how Jaime arrived, that's how José arrived, and now . . .'

'And now?' Eusebio asked. He was beginning to feel worse than bad, the nausea was returning and something was cramping his stomach.

'And now their baby sister is dead.'

'Dead? Sister?'

'Three hours ago, Eusebio, three hours ago. I had a miscarriage.'

Eusebio sat down again and replaced his head in his hands. He didn't notice when José walked into the room.

Again, as though staged by Bunûel, the atmosphere slithered into comic absurdity. José, clothed in baggy pyjamas, came to a halt just inside the doorway and looked in amazement at his parents, at the weird scene they presented, strangers separated by an old wooden table.

Inmaculada was the first to recover and gather her senses.

'José,' she said, standing up and smoothing her clothes, trying to regain composure. 'José, what are you doing?'

'Mama?' José began, uncertainty evident in his shaky voice. 'Mama, what happened? I heard a crash and I heard screaming.' José's wide eyes surveyed the spectacle in front of him, focused on the remains of the shattered plate. 'Something *did* crash, mama. Why . . ?'

92

'It's your father, he's drunk and he dropped the plate,' Inmaculada told him, circumnavigating the truth.

Eusebio looked up and tried to make sense of the way things were unfolding, tried to find some small chink of light in the darkness of his mind before realizing that Inmaculada had already opened the door to another dimension.

'But why the screaming, mama?' José asked. 'It was terrible and it frightened me.'

'I was screaming at him because the plate was one of your aunt's favourites,' Inmaculada explained, embellishing the lie.

'And why's Papa got blood all over his face?' José continued.

'Have I?' Eusebio asked, raising a hand to touch his burning cheeks.

'Yes,' José answered, blunt, direct; contempt showing in his childish voice.

'Must've been the plate,' his father replied, and immediately regretted being so glib. 'How *could* it have been the plate?' he asked himself, realizing he'd have had to have been lying on the floor for the plate to have had any chance of grazing his face.

José was suspicious. 'How?'

'José, I told you,' his mother said sternly. 'Your father is drunk. He dropped the plate, he tried to catch it . . . and he fell to the floor.'

Eusebio rose from the chair and started moving towards his son, feet crunching on shards of broken china.

'José,' he said. 'José, your papi's been stupid and this is the result,' he explained, gesturing towards the mess on the floor. 'This is what happens when someone drinks too much. Let it be a lesson.'

'I don't think José's the one who needs the lesson,' Inmaculada stated in a steely voice, turning towards her husband. 'Do you?'

No one spoke, no one moved, and the sudden shroud of silence became claustrophobic. In order to break the spell, Inmaculada sent José back to his room. 'José, go and get dressed,' she ordered. 'We'll go to the market and leave your father to clean up the mess.'

'Do you think he heard?' Eusebio asked as soon as the boy had shuffled away to get changed.

'He's seven, Eusebio. Of course he heard,' Inmaculada seethed, amazed that her husband failed to understand the mechanics of certainty.

'But do you think he'll re*mem*ber?' Eusebio persisted.

'For a while, Eusebio, for a while.' Inmaculada let her body spill heavily into the chair.

'A while?'

'"Til the next time,' she told him. 'But understand; there had better not *be* a next time.'

Stony-faced, she looked across the table, daring him to make some facetious remark. She peered intently at the face she knew so well and realized she didn't recognize what she saw. The lean, craggy, weather-beaten face with the piercing brown eyes had changed; gone was the devil-may-care expression that she'd loved so much, replaced by something approaching the onset of old age. Eusebio's cheeks had filled out a little, just enough to soften the finely chiselled jaw-line and the high cheekbones that had caused such insane jealousy when other girls had looked admiringly at her Eusebio.

Leaning forward, Inmaculada looked more closely, scrutinizing the face of the man she loved, still loved, despite all his failings. And in the bright morning light, she was able to make out a network of thin red lines, a filigree of crazy paving below blotched skin. Previously unaware of these new additions, she reached out her hand and traced a fingertip through the stubble that, this morning, had not felt the touch of a razor.

6. Lunch

The humming grew louder, accompanied this time by an unholy rattling of something large and metallic.

It was early afternoon, nearly two-thirty, and José had been woken by a strident voice emanating from the television. Suddenly, everything seemed tinny, the newsreader sounding thin and squeaky – although, in part, this was due to the cracked speaker buried inside the old television set – and the approaching Landrover with attendant trailer bouncing over hard ruts, making a noise similar to that of an avenging *Furie.*[25]

The trailer was packed with metallic debris: varying lengths of steel rods, several large sheets of steel mesh, a pair of metal trestles, and various tools – hammers, shovels, jemmies and wrenches. By placing a dozen bags of cement in strategic places, Vicente had made some attempt to keep everything held down, and until the trailer left the smooth surface of the tarmac road, everything had been fine; then, all hell had broken loose. As soon as the vehicle started to negotiate the track's endless twists and turns, potholes and sun-baked corrugations, the constant pitching up and down had caused the heavy cement bags, one by one, to work themselves free.

José stirred himself into slothful action and managed to arrive at the patch of hard standing at the same time as Vicente brought the Landrover to a halt in front of the garage.

'*Niño*,[26] *¿qué pasa?*' José enquired of his son, pointing with his stick at the scrambled devastation barely contained within the confines of the trailer.

Vicente jumped out of the cab, grinning widely. '*No te preocupes*,[27] *papa*. Since when has it been possible to transport stuff along these lanes without a little shake-up?'

'Hah,' José grumbled, throwing an arm around the young man's shoulders. Together they walked to the patio and sat at the table in front of the flickering television set.

'Still going on, then?' Vicente asked, sipping at a can of beer.

'It'll be going on 'til doomsday,' José answered. 'And that's probably not so far away.'

9/11, as it had been labelled, both fascinated and repelled José, and he would willingly have engaged in earnest discussion about the whys and wherefores but, just as he opened his mouth, he looked up to see María sailing towards him, a huge smile on her face and a large earthenware dish in her hands.

'Okay boys,' she said, lowering the steaming concoction onto the table. 'Lunch.'

María clasped her hands – still encased in the enormous protective pads of a pair of oven gloves – together, creating a sort of damp muffled thud, and winked at Vicente. 'Your favourite,' she told him.

'Rabbit stew?' he asked politely, playing the mother-and-son game so much loved and appreciated by María.

'Rabbit stew, your favourite,' she corroborated, beaming

and blinking in ecstasy before sighing and turning to head back into the kitchen.

'I love rabbit stew, mama,' came Vicente's dutiful response.

Father and son exchanged glances and returned to the serious matter of emptying beer cans.

'You know Pepe's been told he can't continue with his house?' Vicente informed his father. 'You know, that half-finished construction to the right of the track?'

'You mean where it forks off towards Canillas?'

'No no, the other one, before the fork; I'd forgotten there were two, of course there are two.' Vicente took a gulp of beer and placed the can on the table, sliding it to and fro, demonstrating a bend in the track. 'Here,' he said, stabbing a finger inside the imaginary hairpin. 'It's here, where the land slopes up to the right.'

'Oh, that one?' José responded vaguely. 'That's Pepe's?'

'Come on papi, you know it is. We've talked about this on numerous occasions, remember?'

'The illegal one?' José asked, brightening up. 'Pepe, who never bothers with the paperwork?'

'Well, he does and he doesn't,' Vicente agreed.

'Did he or didn't he?' José asked, always a stickler for having his information just so.

'He did,' Vicente replied. 'He went to the *ayuntamiento*[28] and submitted the plans which he'd drawn himself, and because he was a hundred percent certain they'd give him permission, he started.'

'To build?' José queried, sensing somewhere in his brain that this was ancient history and adding as an afterthought, 'Obviously.'

María arrived back at the table and set down a plate of

chunky bread and a dish of gleaming potatoes. She started ladling generous helpings of stew.

'Obviously,' Vicente asserted.

'Without permission?'

'Well, yes.'

'But   '

'But he knew there'd be no problem,' Vicente went on to explain, taking hold of the plate proffered by his mother. 'There's never been a problem. People have been busily building houses all over the mountains, nonstop.'

'Until now,' José said seriously.

'Until now,' Vicente agreed.

He forked some of the food into his mouth. 'Very good, mama,' he adjudicated round a piece of hot rabbit. 'Excellent!'

It was a foregone conclusion. María's rabbit stew was venerated for miles around, it was her *pièce de résistance*, but still it needed to be acknowledged. José looked at his wife and mumbled something vaguely optimistic.

María believed she was in paradise. She loved it when Vicente stopped by for a meal, it expanded the daily gathering by fifty percent and made the whole process of preparation more encouragingly worthwhile; and this past week he'd been around nearly every day. She looked fondly at the two men in her life, Vicente and his father, sitting at the table, putting the world to rights. Sometimes, although not very often, José's elder brother Jaime would bring his wife along, and María would be as happy as a pygmy in a doll's house, running about with plates of food and listening and occasionally joining in with the conversation. She didn't know too much about construction or rules and regulations, and most of the time was content to be a silent spectator, chef-supreme in her world far removed from matters so mundane.

'Until now,' Vicente repeated. 'It's all changed. According to Pepe, the mayor keeps telling him that it's not his fault.'

'Pepe's?' José asked, a little confused.

'What? No,' Vicente replied. 'The mayor's.'

'What's not the mayor's fault?' José asked, a little more confused.

'More?' María asked, placing a ladleful of stew onto Vicente's barely touched plate.

Thrown by the interruption, the men looked up, briefly surprised, briefly uncertain. They watched as María's ladle performed the same trick of replenishment, depositing another helping of stew onto José's plate.

'All these changes,' Vicente answered, watching a couple of boiled potatoes land on his plate, courtesy of the flying ladle. 'It's getting more and more difficult,' he expounded.

'Well, whose fault *is* it?' José asked.

'According to what the mayor told Pepe, it's the *Junta's*.[29]

'What's it got to do with them?'

'According to . . .'

'Don't worry about who said what,' José said, agitated and impatient. 'Just tell me, in anybody's words, why the *Junta* is involving itself in matters that it shouldn't.'

'Accord . . . Ecology,' Vicente answered.

'Ecology?'

'I think that's the word,' Vicente hesitated. 'It's something to do with the land, I think.'

'Ecology,' José repeated, savouring the sound of the new word. 'Ecology.'

'According . . . The *Junta* thinks all this construction is bad for the land.'

'Ecology,' José had become stuck in the rarely explored world of academe.

'We're taking too much out,' Vicente continued, trying to remember everything that Pepe had told him. 'And not putting enough back,' he concluded.

'What are you talking about?' María asked, bored, having ceased operations with the ladle.

'Ecology,' José advised, proud of his newly acquired knowledge.

'Gravel and sand and marble,' Vicente enthused, warming to the subject as his mind groped along Pepe's half-forgotten sentences. 'We're taking too much out of the land,' he repeated.

'So?' José asked.

'We're destroying the . . . Environment.' Vicente answered, grinning widely, suddenly happy having remembered the word he realized he should have used earlier.

José pointed at the flickering screen which, yet again, had decided to display the grim pictures of two towers enveloped in ever expanding clouds of flame-streaked smoke. 'And these people? What are they doing?' he asked the assembled duo. 'What the hell do they think they're doing?'

'They're fighting for their freedom,' Vicente answered.

'Freedom?' José exploded. 'What the fuck do they care about freedom? That's not what this is all about.'

'What *is* it about, then?' Vicente asked somewhat reluctantly, knowing the question would send his father on a marathon of world history.

'It's about a bunch of malcontents,' José explained. 'Religious zealots, whose one aim in life is to convert the rest of the world and bring it into line with their blinkered way of thinking.'

'By attacking America?' Vicente asked, perplexed.

'By attacking anyone not of their creed,' José said. 'It'll be us next, I expect. In fact I don't know why we haven't already been attacked.'

'Us? Spain?'

'Yep. Especially down here in the south, al-Andalus as it used to be called. Don't forget that Córdoba used to be the hub of the Muslim world, Granada and Sevilla as well, until of course they got kicked out in the fifteenth century by Ferdinand and Isabella.'

'But, papa, that was hundreds of years ago, before even you were born!' Vicente pointed out.

'People have long memories,' José stated.

'Hmm . . . I suppose.'

Vicente rummaged through scraps of vague information, snippets of gossip from late nights in the pub. 'A little like Gibraltar, then?' he threw into the sticky afternoon heat.

'Gibraltar?'

'Yes, papa, it's ours, it's part of the mainland and we want it back.'

'True, but it's not quite the same thing.'

'What about Ceuta and Melilla, then?' Vicente asked, pursuing the course of the righteous. 'That's the same sort of thing. The Moroccans want to kick *us* out.'

'Yes, but it's different.'

'How different, papi, how different?'

'Our squabbles with the English and the Moroccans are about territory, about treaties, agreements and gov . . .'

'Exactly,' Vicente beamed, vindication within reach.

'The mess in America, though, is a result of religion and fervent belief. Niceties and the luxury of diplomatic negotiations don't come into it. History, *niño*, history, it tends to repeat itself, until something like this comes along and turns everything on its head.'

José paused and looked at the ruined castle across the valley and at the hillsides with their endless terraces held behind snug ramparts, stone buttresses holding everything together. 'There are reminders everywhere you look,' he added moodily. He picked up his knife and fork and bisected a boiled potato.

'It's a bit stupid though, isn't it?' Vicente pondered. 'I mean, it's like . . .'

'Putting your hand in the lion's cage?' José suggested.

'Exactly,' Vicente agreed. 'Who'd be so crazy?'

'I know who,' José answered, warming to the subject he'd spent most of the week thinking about. 'I know exactly who, and they're destabilizing the world. You talk about the *Junta* and the fanciful ideas it dreams up in a couple of offices in Sevilla, but this . . .' he pointed at the television set. 'Mark my words, this'll change everything.'

'How do you mean, papa?' Vicente asked.

'Well,' José paused while he tried to think of something, anything.

'Well?' Vicente pushed.

'All those aircraft that stopped flying, what did they call it? . . . Grounded, that's what they were . . . Well, that's never happened before. Worldwide too, big reductions in travel, *big* reductions.'

'Yes, but that was just for safety, they didn't know what was going on.'

'And that just about sums it up,' José agreed. 'They don't know what's going on, *niño,* no one *does*!'

In the still of the afternoon, when nothing had the will or the strength to move, a voice called from the steep slopes of the drying pans.

'José!'

José lifted his glass to his lips and raised his eyes to heaven.

'José!' the voice came again.

José tapped Vicente on his arm, grinned and responded, '*Qué?*'

María appeared in fits and starts, a black rotundity scrambling over the brow of bank beneath the terrace.

'Can't you hear it?' she asked, panting. 'What's the matter with you? What *is* that noise?'

'What noise?' José asked, looking at his wife, then at his son.

'Listen,' María exhorted.

The men sat, heads to one side like puppets waiting for someone to pull their strings.

'There,' María told them. 'There it is, something like a seagull, but strange.'

'Maybe it *is* a seagull?' José suggested, unimpressed, uninterested.

'No, silly; it's too loud, too weird.'

'A rabbit then, maybe it's a rabbit?' José tried, wondering at his wife's consternation.

'A rabbit?' María asked, wondering at José's reasoning, wondering at the lack of it.

'Caught by a dog, or a polecat,' José explained, hoisting

himself from the chair to accompany Vicente to the Landrover.

Hands on hips, red-faced, María stared at the ground and pondered the possibility; and then it came again, the sound she found so perplexing, and this time José heard it too.

'That *is* strange,' José admitted, turning towards the direction from which the noise seemed to travel. 'Come on,' he said, 'let's investigate.'

'Do you need me?' Vicente called from the Landrover.

'No no, go on and get those beams arranged,' José smiled at his son. 'I think we'll be okay, unless it's a very *big* seagull.'

'Or a monster rabbit,' Vicente suggested, grinning through the window as his foot released the clutch.

Grasping his stick in his right hand, José placed his left arm loosely around María's shoulders and thus they stood, silhouetted against silent swirling dust, watching the vehicle lurch along the track until it disappeared from view.

'It's the wrong time of day, José,' María told him. 'Rabbits don't come out until dusk.'

'Must be a seagull, then,' José chuckled. 'A big one.'

Fifteen minutes later, they were on the track, following it through an almond grove before it levelled out to curve round the hillside above an avocado plantation. José was in a good mood, always happy when wandering through the countryside, despite the hilly and often steep terrain. Using his stick, he pointed at objects near and far, up and down, and had an anecdote for nearly all of them. After a while, he indicated the stream far below, a mere trickle winding along the bottom of a gully.

'Less and less,' he told María. 'We need rain, lots of rain, and heavy.' He pointed his stick at the avocado trees. 'Look María, look how droopy those leaves are, and look how dull.'

'But Manolo waters them every other day,' María ventured. 'Doesn't he?'

'Maybe he does, maybe he doesn't,' José answered. 'And every time Manolo opens the tap, down goes the water level, further and further. They say that wells are having to be drilled deeper and deeper, to five or six hundred metres, and when all the underground supplies are used up, that'll be it.' He waved his stick in the air, gesturing at the trees, at the hills, at the valley and everything in it. 'We need rain,' he finished, and kicked a pebble over the edge of the track.

María stepped forward and watched the pebble as it bounced down the slope between the wilting trees, and then she raised her head at the sound of the creature they'd come to investigate. The noise was coming from further down the hill, but a little more to the west. Doubling back on themselves, José and María followed a path leading diagonally downwards across the side of the hill, bringing them eventually to an ancient water deposit.

'Of course!' José exclaimed. 'The fierce beast will be stuck in the deposit.'

The path seemed to continue further down the slope and below the deposit, so José and María left the track and clambered across rough ground to the upper enclosing wall. Approaching through the undergrowth, they heard the noise again, louder, reverberating within the enclosed space. Up close, the sound was diabolical, as though someone or something was being subjected to mediaeval torture. María stopped, looked at José as if seeking assurance and grabbed his hand as they peered over the lip of the ruined construction. It was deep, maybe four or five metres, and empty, save for a few inches of murky green liquid forming a thick scum, its surface broken here and there by dead branches and slime-encrusted boulders.

'Look!' cried José. 'There, over there in the corner, see?'

María scanned the bottom of the tank. 'I don't see anything,' she said.

'On that rock, brown, in the corner,' José pointed. 'Look, it's moving.'

Having been discovered, the animal decided to shriek again, the sound decidedly that of a toad.

'It's a toad, José, it's a toad,' María whispered. 'What are we going to do?'

'I don't know,' José replied, staring at the amphibian. 'I can't get down and it can't get up.'

María leaned further forwards and noticed some rungs set into the side of the tank. She leaned back and stood up, pensively folding her arms. 'José, you could climb down there and rescue it.'

'Crazy woman,' José guffawed. 'Look at those rungs, look how rusty they are. And the brickwork doesn't look too good, either.' He peered into the gloomy depths and banged his stick against one of the rungs. Much to his surprise the rung held firm, so he struck at another and one end of the metal bracket broke away from the wall, pieces of brick and cement falling into the stagnant water, making a noise as of rocks dropping into mud. José grinned at some long-lost boyhood memory, something that revolved around the same sounds and the same sticky consistency of sand and sea, a porridge-like mixture, soggy and somehow satisfying. He climbed onto the retaining wall and sat there, his short little legs dangling over the edge. María moved up behind him and flicked some dust from the decrepit brickwork. The toad croaked as though clearing its throat, waiting for some decisive action from the humans.

'What does it mean?' María asked nervously. 'What's it all about?'

'The toad?' José queried in amazement. 'We'll wait until tomorrow, bring Vicente and a bucket.'

'The attack, José, the planes, the towers . . . and all those people.'

'What does it mean?' José echoed. 'What does it mean?' He kicked his heels against the inside wall and sent a shower of brick dust into the green swamp. 'It means the world will never be the same again. It means an impossible situation. It means that terrorists can attack where and when they want, no warning, no hesitation, no compunction; it's a free-for-all. The world's become unstable, so much hatred, so much jealousy and suspicion; it's a powder keg waiting for some lunatic to come along and light the fuse.' José kicked the wall and more dust shimmered crimson as it filtered through the sun's rays. He turned and smiled at his companion, his María, his squat round beautiful wife. 'For us, my love, I don't think we'll see too much change. We'd need another revolution, another civil war to affect our way of life.' He looked up at the ridge on the far side of the valley, at the outline of the castle, jagged ruins stark against the sunlight. He picked up his stick and tapped it gently against the side of his face. 'I think we're safe,' he grinned. 'For now.'

In the heat of the afternoon, the climb back to the cottage was an arduous event, necessitating numerous halts so that José could regain his breath. During one such halt, María told her husband about a problem with the outside drain, how it seemed to take forever for water to disappear into the system of pipes that led eventually to the cesspit.

'It's those damned dogs,' José muttered, 'infernal things. They're always moulting and leaving great hanks of hair all over the patio, that's what it'll be. If you swept the place more often,' he grumbled, 'it wouldn't have a chance to clog up the drains.'

'I sweep every day,' María retorted, 'but you're so busy sleeping all the time, you don't notice.'

'Huh,' José wheezed, leaning for support against the trunk of an almond tree.

'Beer, food and sleep, that's all you know,' María informed him, looking up into the tree at an outcrop of nuts that had missed the previous year's harvest.

'Tomorrow,' José said. 'I'll look at the drain tomorrow.'

'*Mañana, mañana; siempre mañana,*[30] María chortled. '*Hombre*, tomorrow is going to be a busy day, what with the frog and the drains.'

'Yeah yeah,' José responded, puce and breathing heavily. 'Vicente'll help me, he's a good lad, not like some of the others.'

María purred at the mention of her son's name. 'Yes,' she said, clasping her hands in front of her small circular body, 'and we can all have lunch together. I'll prepare something special.'

'*¡Joder! ¿Mujer, qué pasa contigo?*[31] José asked, looking up through tired eyes. 'You're always preparing something special. You prepared something special today, you prepared something special yesterday.'

'Well, maybe tomorrow it'll be something extra special,'

María told him enigmatically.

José shook his head in abstraction and levered himself away from the tree. 'Come on then, I need my siesta.'

7. *Enriqueta*

Not knowing exactly what to expect, José felt apprehensive. Last year, so he'd been told, he was too young, but at the ripe old age of seven, his parents deemed him old enough to attend the proceedings.

The pig was huge, and as he stood staring at it, José remembered the occasions when he'd helped his dad feed the animal, recalling his amazement at how much food it consumed; that, and the fact that the pig never had any exercise, he knew, accounted for its size. He smiled, thinking back to the day at the tail end of winter, when his father had brought the animal home.

The piglet had been tethered into a cart and hauled along behind a mule, and the proud expression on Eusebio's face had been there for all to see. The family had gathered round as his father untied the ropes fastening the cart's long wooden arms to each side of the mule, and then had helped lower the back of the cart until it touched the ground, its two empty arms pointing skyward. Obeying gravity, the pig had slithered earthwards, spindly legs and baby trotters sliding helplessly on the smooth wooden boards. But, much to the amusement of the onlookers, the halter had been too short and the animal was left standing, hind-legs on the ground, body and forelegs supported against the upended cart. Terrified at the situation in which it found itself, the wretched animal had squealed loudly, forcing José to cover his ears against such onslaught. It was the first time he'd witnessed such a noise, but in comparison to the tumult currently emanating from the sty, the whining dogs and the circle of guilty spectators, it had been nothing.

José looked at the collection of people standing around – his brother, his mother and his father, his uncles and aunts; it was an extensive family and today was special, a day of celebration. Today, the whole family was in attendance. It was the day of the pig, the day of Enriqueta.

It happened every year, once, sometimes twice, and the family declared it to be a day of fiesta, a holiday, and therefore nobody worked. The visiting relatives arrived with flagons of wine, baskets of bread, cheese, and any other offerings they could lay their hands on. They arrived with their spouses, their lovers, their babies, their mothers and fathers, and their grumbling grandparents. They arrived on their mules or their horses and some, having traversed several kilometres of sunbaked hilly terrain on foot, arrived hot and dusty. Some arrived resplendent in their new metal acquisition, a car, and issued proudly from every door, beaming and gleaming with pride, passengers and car alike. The rest of the family gathered itself around the steaming lump of metal as it wheezed and hummed with life until the owner, almost beside himself with good humour, found the will to switch off the engine.

José found himself to be in a strange sort of mood. He

ran around sniggering at everyone and when they looked to see what he was up to, scampered off to snigger at somebody else. It was the uncertainty of knowing, or rather not knowing what he should be doing. Having been given no tasks to carry out, he felt rejected, unacknowledged, free to roam on the periphery of something tangible but just out of reach.

For four or five months the beast had been incarcerated in a small shed, a place of purgatory measured in semi-darkness, the only source of light entering via a barred ventilation panel set high in the steel door.

The squealing was overwhelming, almost contagious, and José looked at his father, trying to catch his eye, hoping to establish for himself that all was as it should be; although at this particular moment he reckoned he was more terrified than the pig.

Eusebio went to the shed and furtively opened the door, and after a brief struggle, managed to attach a length of rope around one of the pig's front legs. The look of sheer terror on the animal's face as it was hauled into the afternoon sun, contrasted horribly with the smug satisfaction that sat on the face of the human. The assembled crowd started to clap and cheer, those near enough smacking the beast on its flanks as though somehow congratulating the unfortunate animal for attaining such a magnificent girth.

José watched his father lead the porker around the small area of scrappy land, wincing whenever the overweight creature, due to too much pressure being applied to the rope, was made to skitter about on three legs.

'Papa, what are you doing?' José yelled. 'Look, you're holding the rope too tight.' His high-pitched voice cut through the heat of the day, but the onlookers, caught up in visceral excitement, paid no attention.

'Hey,' he screamed. 'Be careful.'

Eusebio, tearing his eyes from the heavyweight prize at the end of the halter, looked up. 'Don't you worry 'bout that my son, old porker don't mind; least if she does, she won't have to worry much longer.' He laughed out loud and the attendant throng cackled obscene support.

José smiled weakly. He knew the pig was due to meet its end today and his pals had told him conflicting rumours about what would happen, but he felt sorry for the beast and was angry at the way it was being treated. Enriqueta was part of the family, a fixture, an everyday ritual of feed and water, and now his father wanted to kill her.

At a sign from his father, José's brother and one of his uncles, the owner of the car, stepped forward and helped to push the pig onto its side, then rolled it onto its back. One of the men let out a howl when a flailing trotter gouged a furrow into the back of his hand. Blood rose quickly to the surface and the wounded man lashed out in blind fury, smashing his fist into the pig's unprotected nose. The animal reared its head backwards, causing another of the trio to topple forwards and crash onto the body of the original protagonist. Each man had a length of cord in his hands and working quickly, tied the animal's legs together, two at the front, and then the two rear ones. Like a fish out of water, Enriqueta slewed to and fro, trying to evade the ropes that were being pulled ever tighter.

And now, a new dimension was added to the mêlée, a noise, a high-pitched keening from the tick-infested dogs. Animalistic senses aware of impending danger, the milling canines raised their hideous black-lipped snouts and gave vent to anguish.

'Jesus,' José said to himself. Then again, 'Jesus Christ!' He said it louder, much louder, stamping his feet on the ground to attract attention. 'Somebody do something,' he demanded, wild eyed.

But no one did. They did nothing except laugh while the poor animal rolled around on its back, flailing its bound legs helplessly back and forth. After attaching the cords to its legs, José's dad, along with his brother and uncle, had let go of the beast and now it was writhing about like a creature demented, all the while squealing tremendously and, it seemed to José, staring at him fixedly through little pink eyes.

In vain, José tried to shut out the sound. Bad enough when the baby pig had arrived nine months ago, now, the banshees had been let loose and the air was sucked inside out, the atmosphere rent asunder.

For Enriqueta, it was too much. Overwhelming fear and wild indignation at finding herself hogtied and helpless, led to a loosening of muscles, and a stream of piss and liquid excrement issued from the terrified animal. Almost immediately, the acute stench infiltrated the olfactory systems of all present, especially the dogs, whose mounting cacophony brought them to the edge of nervous meltdown. A squadron of flies, lured by the sweat of toiling men and the rapture of stamping in pools of urine and feculent material, materialized from nowhere, jostling incessantly in shape shifting harmony.

'For Christ's sake,' José yelled, rushing towards the struggling animal.

In a trice, his brother caught hold of him and hauled him out of harm's way. José strained at the enforced leash of Jaime's arms. It was a pointless struggle, equal to that of Enriqueta. Jaime was twelve, tall and gangly, almost grown up, almost a man, and with the manual labour associated with helping his father run the homestead, his dark sinewy arms were like bands of steel. José realized he was going nowhere but, damned if he was going to give up his support for the animal he'd taken so much trouble to care for, remembered he still had his voice.

'*¿De qué vas?*[32] he screamed at the men surrounding the pig. 'Let her go!'

Enriqueta seemed to pick up on José's shouting, seemed to understand that at least one of these crazy humans was on her side, and, wriggling furiously against her bondage, squealed all the louder.

Losing command of the situation, Eusebio was at a loss. 'José!' he yelled, '*¡cállate!*[33] Christ, he thought, here I am, surrounded by family and friends for this day of celebration, with my son up in arms and causing trouble. '*I'm* supposed to be the man in charge of proceedings,' he told himself, striding purposefully towards his young son.

'José,' he snapped at the youngster. 'This is *my* day. This is a special day for all the family.' He looked at José's face, saw the tears streaming down the boy's cheeks, and lost control. Raising his right hand, he delivered a stinging slap to the side of José's head. In the ensuing silence, José, feeling his brother's arms relinquish their hold, realized he had a choice – run, or stay where he was. Although frightened of his father, he was determined not to show weakness and thus chose the latter option.

'José,' his father screamed. 'You bring shame to your father and to your family. If you can't be a man, go. Go and shut yourself in the *cortijo*. Go, get out of my sight.'

During this passionate one-sided debate, Enriqueta had

sensed that someone else was in serious trouble and now, with the assembled crowd beginning nervously to chatter amongst itself, reckoned she might as well scale down her cries for help.

José, face burning, eyes brimming, slouched away, kicking out at the orbiting dogs that were quivering in anticipation of some frenzied killing. Halfway to the cottage, he changed his mind and changed direction, walking instead towards the tall eucalyptus tree. He stopped next to the peeling papery trunk and sat in the shade of its parched leaves. In front of him, across the narrow valley, a horse and rider glided majestically along the ridge and José became transfixed by their steady progress, each rising hoof lifting small clouds of dust that flickered momentarily in the sunlight before drifting into nothingness. Behind him, the intermittent squeals of the incensed animal brought him back to rude reality. In his young untainted innocence, José knew what these people were up to – cruelty, pure and simple; inhumanity run amok. He trusted no one and even suspected that these barbarians, wound up and intoxicated with bloodlust, might come looking for *him*. He stood and positioned himself behind the tree, and from the safety of this vantage point, craned his head sideways so that he could see what was going on.

Everyone was drinking and laughing, raising glasses and shouting '*¡Salud!*'[34] They'd formed a circle around Enriqueta, *his* Enriqueta, who lay trembling in terror, all tied up and wallowing in her own filth, unable to stand, unable to escape these mad revellers, these unholy tormentors.

It had been March or April when Enriqueta had arrived, perhaps even February, José couldn't remember which, and the young pig, only two months old, had been loosely tethered with a long piece of rope, giving ample opportunity to roam and forage for grass, weeds and leaves. José had been given the job of caring for the animal, for making sure there was always water in her trough and for supplementing her diet with scraps of food left over from Inmaculada's kitchen.

He'd been responsible also for coming up with the name, Enriqueta, after a girl he was hopelessly in love with at school. His father had informed him that the pig was female, so José, unable to lavish love and attention upon the girl of his dreams, devoted himself to the four-legged version of the unattainable Enriqueta. The two had enjoyed long conversations, albeit a little one-sided, about everything; and while José had wandered happily about the dry countryside with the pig as constant companion, he'd talked to, embraced, and scratched the animal's back at every opportunity. He liked to think that Enriqueta, the pig, understood; and because the animal appeared to smile at him every time she looked up from snuffling inspection of the sparse yet intensely interesting undergrowth, he became convinced.

José had never told Enriqueta, the schoolgirl, about his porcine friend and hoped fervently that no one else had – he'd thought it would be too difficult to explain.

A sudden breeze shimmied through the dry leaves, rippling and rustling, bringing with it a sickly pungent odour of fear. Intermittent light flashed across the open space, causing José to look up and notice the reflections bouncing from a large tin bowl that his mother was carrying. She was moving slowly, deliberately, her passage across the uneven ground accompanied by the sound of metal against metal. José narrowed his eyes and tried to see through the dancing points of light, the jangling brilliance that was keeping step with Inmaculada's wary progress. He blinked and focused, blinked and focused, and saw a knife, long and deadly, and it was this that with each measured step was clanking against the bowl.

At Inmaculada's approach, the onlookers parted, allowing access to the trussed pig. Eusebio reached forward, took the knife from his wife's hand and tested its keenness by rubbing his thumb along the blade. Apparently satisfied, he bent down and placed his strong forearm around the animal's snout, pulling Enriqueta's head back and upwards while Inmaculada positioned the bowl on the bare earth below the pig's outstretched neck.

Someone, José thought it was his uncle Jorge, had lowered himself to kneel on the animal's flank, pinning it to the ground, and Jaime had attached himself to the cord that bound the pig's hind legs, pulling for all his worth, trying to prevent the flailing legs from getting in the way. Someone else was doing the same with Enriqueta's front legs; it was grotesque, there was nothing the wretched animal could do.

A sudden fat unhealthy silence descended and hung heavily over the macabre spectacle, as Enriqueta, sensing defeat, stopped squealing and tensed her body into rigid immobility. It was a breath frozen in time; leaves ceased to stir, flies stopped buzzing, insects put a hold on their busy activities, and the dogs stood about in uncertain attitudes, looking at one another, tails curled between trembling legs.

Enriqueta's days of freedom had ended in early summer when she'd been incarcerated in the shed. Constructed from breeze blocks and roofed with a rusty sheet of corrugated iron, it was no more than a cell, maybe two-and-a-half metres by one-and-a-half, Enriqueta's very own black hole of Calcutta.

José had railed against his father. 'Why?' he'd asked. 'Why does she have to stay in there?'

And as June rolled effortlessly into July, José had continued his vociferous fight for the pig's freedom. 'It's like a dungeon in there, papa,' he'd informed Eusebio, 'and the smell is . . .'

'Enriqueta can't be allowed to roam, José,' his father had told him bluntly.

'Why?'

The answer, aimed at bringing the troublesome conversation to a halt, had been precise. 'She has to start putting on weight, and that's not going to happen if she spends all day wandering around the *campo*, is it? Too much exercise.'

'But she can hardly turn round and there's no air. It's like an oven,' José protested.

'José!' Eusebio yelled. 'Enriqueta stays in the shed.'

'But . . .'

'No buts,' he was told, firmly.

There was no option, and the only way in which José was able to assuage his conscience, was to continue in his role as the animal's benefactor. He continued to hold lengthy conversations with Enriqueta and did his best to keep the sty as clean as possible. This was quite a difficult task on account of the habitat being so small, but José found a way to work around the pig, managing to rake out all the soiled litter and replace it with forkfuls of fresh, golden, sun-warmed straw.

Along with her living arrangements, Enriqueta's diet also had been changed. The countryside was parched and vegetation thin on the ground, so even if Enriqueta had retained the freedom to roam, she'd have had to rely on prickly pears from the strange-looking big-eared cactus plants and, later in the season, acorns and figs which dropped in abundance from over-tired trees seeking relief. Every day, José would scurry around filling a large shallow dish with these epicurean delights, adding handfuls of husks saved from last year's harvest and chunks of dried up grape-skins plundered from tottering stacks of rounds, discarded and forgotten after the pressing process. It was amazing how quickly the pig had expanded but José understood that, with nowhere to go and with no exercise, this was normal. In retrospect, he learned that his father had been correct.

Just this morning, when he'd ventured forth to give Enriqueta her breakfast, she'd been facing towards the metal door, and now, as he thought about it, he realized she'd been facing in exactly the same direction for weeks. Suddenly it dawned upon him that it wasn't just her eagerness to see him or to receive her food that caused her always to be looking towards the gate, it was simply that she was stuck, unable to turn.

As comprehension filtered slowly through his brain, José began to realize he'd been the architect of Enriqueta's demise. He, and he alone, had been responsible for the daily feeding of the caged animal. Sometimes he'd gone out of his way to find special titbits; and sometimes, caught in the act of scraping tasty morsels from the family's dinner plates, he'd incurred his mother's wrath. In his innocence he'd accepted the job, had fallen upon the duty with pride in his heart; and Enriqueta had been lavished with unbridled love and attention. Through his anguish and his tears, José came to understand that he'd been duped. His father had impressed upon him the importance of the task and now he knew where that importance lay, where it had always lain, for each long drawn out month. His parents had tricked him, had fooled him into believing he was doing good, and daily they'd encouraged him in his friendship with Enriqueta. Now, in his rage, he saw the betrayal for what it was – his betrayal of the pig, and the betrayal played out by his folks. He stepped out from behind the tree and marched towards the circle of silence.

A flash of sunlight fled from the knife as it sliced through skin, flesh and artery. Bright crimson blood splashed into the metal bowl and Enriqueta's bound legs thrashed frantically, as muscles and heart, still active, still functioning, combined to pump the precious stream of life. José, watching as if in a dream, saw the strain evident on his father's face as Eusebio clung with all his might to the pig's head. The sound of blood spurting against metal was obscene but was soon drowned under an avalanche of demented howling from the dogs. It was a nightmare played out in harsh reality beneath an uncaring sun. Long seconds stretched into eternity, and then the bowl beneath Enriqueta's neck had to be replaced and a fresh sea of warm red blood was delivered into mankind's waiting hands. Eventually, the blood ceased to flow; eventually, the heart stopped beating; eventually, Enriqueta died and was hacked to pieces. The animal, once so proud, strong and noble, disappeared, as it were, in front of José's red-rimmed eyes. Enriqueta's head, with its sweet face and short smiling snout, was sundered from her body and grotesquely held aloft by José's father, who seemed to relish the drops of blood that fell through the air to land on his radiant half-crazed face. At that instant and for the first time in his life, José experienced hatred and an intense desire to become disassociated from humanity and all it stood for.

Moments later, the scrubby yard became a flurry of activity. Uncle Jorge picked up the dispatching-knife and, drawing a line from throat to tail, slit open the warm pink carcass. It was as though some pre-ordained signal had been given, and received, the attendants ready to carry out their well-rehearsed duties.

Each and every part of the pig's anatomy disassembled into thin air; the blades were out and being wielded with practiced precision. Enriqueta's eyes, ears, nose, tongue and trotters were put into a large *puchero*[35] to become part of a stew that would last for days. Her head was placed in another pot and left to simmer, sedate dissolution enriching the bubbling waters to form a rich, tasty stock. Enriqueta's entrails, hanging out of the gaping wound, were cut free and then gathered and sloshed into waiting buckets which the women picked up and carried away. Eusebio, having told Jaime to take the bowls of blood into the cottage, started to work on the carcass and soon began handing various chunks of meat to the other men, who set about cutting them into smaller portions.

José sat on the ground in the dusty haze of late afternoon. He was angry and bewildered and didn't know what to do. Then he realized there was nothing he *could* do; it was over. He became angry at himself for not having tried to help Enriqueta in her struggle to be free. He'd never forget the sound of her screams as the cords had been placed around her short stubby legs, and he'd never forget the little piggy smile that had still been evident on the detached head.

Getting to his feet, he scuffed his way across the site of desecration and scowled at the dogs, silent in their awareness of being suddenly unnecessary. Frustration trapped José in a mood of indecision, he was rudderless and without a friend in the world, and then, catching sight of the women heading towards the setting sun, he determined to follow them. Cantering along the track until only a few paces behind the feminine train, he slowed his pace and ambled along in their footsteps, accompanied by the noise of chatter and grinding metal as the buckets swung to-and-fro in their iron handles. Following a long curve to the left, the cavalcade passed through an area of olive trees before descending steeply into the valley's welcoming shade. The women and their buckets soon reached their destination, grouping at a point in the track where it led into a stream.

Inmaculada clicked her tongue. 'Every year it gets smaller,' she said, pointing at the compacted earth on either side of the brook. 'Look, you can make out last year's water level.'

While the women shook their heads in shared dismay, José ventured to edge of the gully to get a better look. The crust of dried earth crumbled away and José pitched headlong into the shallow water. And there he sat, feeling stupid, pinned beneath the cackles of female laughter until one of the women stepped forward and José looked up to see his aunt, his wonderful favourite aunt Rosie, jumping into the rivulet to give him a helping hand.

With the boy out of the way, the rest of the women stepped into the stream and began their task of cleaning Enriqueta's entrails. José decided to leave them to it, he'd had enough for one day, more than enough, and turning away, started the long wearisome climb back to the top of the hill.

He'd just reached the area by the olive trees when something caused him to look to his left, towards the ancient castle and the distant sea. A flash of lightning, brighter than the sun, filled the horizon and José waited for the rumble of thunder that he knew had to follow. But it didn't, there was no thunder. He'd seen storms before, lots of them, and at this time of year they were frequent visitors to the lofty mountain corridors where they'd crash about for hours, hurling the abuse of gods. José stopped in his tracks. Just a minute, he thought, there haven't *been* any storms this year, there's been no rain, *nada!* He looked up as another flash sizzled through the early evening air, and shook his head when again there was no resounding crack of thunder. Strange, he thought, before coming to the conclusion that the storm must be so far away as to make the crashes inaudible.

Approaching the *cortijo*, he encountered the menfolk occupied in busy preparation at the outdoor grill. There was much shouting and laughter, a screen of drunken revelry to ward off the dying of the day, the ending of Enriqueta's day. José decided there was no way he'd partake in the feast on Enriqueta's flesh, he wanted to absolve himself and be absent from this morbid celebration. Having resolved to go indoors and shut himself away, he looked up as lightning once again filled the skies. This time, the sheet lightning was accompanied by several searing streaks of fork lightning, the spectacular display throwing the scene around the grill into distorted silhouette. José blinked, and in momentary blindness, perceived images of devils dancing round the fires of hell were etched into the back of his eyelids. Yelling in alarm at visions of Dante, he stumbled towards the open front door, his presence unseen and unnoticed. He staggered along the short corridor and entered the first room on the left, his bedroom, his place of refuge, and, removing his shoes, threw himself onto the bed. He lay in the gloom, a strange yellow syrupy twilight, and while wondering about the storm that surely was about to break out of its pent-up silence, tried mentally to scrape the frightening pictures from his frazzled vision.

He must have dozed, because when at last he opened his eyes to the surrounding darkness, it took a few moments for him to become fully aware of the strange flutelike sounds that probably had been the cause of his waking. He sat up on the small bed and peered through the heavy black atmosphere, managing eventually to see the tiny window outlined against flickering illumination from an external lantern. The sound became louder, steadily growing in intensity until the noise of rustling trees made it clear that the original whimper had been caused by wind.

A loud clatter from outside brought José to his feet and he padded to the front door, which swung open as though in salutation. Running a bare foot along the edge of the corridor, he located the brick used as a doorstop and slid it into position, then, with hands holding onto the frame, stood in the open doorway and surveyed the scene. The lantern, sheltered in a corner of the patio, shed enough light for José to see that one of the plastic chairs had been tossed aside and was lying on its back, nestled against the low retaining wall. He looked up into dim shadows, where the lower branches of the trees bordering the drying pans were swaying violently, tormented by the gale.

'¿José, qué haces?'[36]

His father's voice came from behind, out of the darkness.
'Nada papa. No hago nada.'[37]

José didn't move from his position in the doorway, he just stood there, absorbed in his observation of the power of nature. His father moved closer and put a huge hand on José's left shoulder.

'It's the voice of the gods,' José said.

'What?' asked Eusebio.

'The voice of the gods,' José repeated, turning to look at his father.

Eusebio shook his head and a vivid tongue of lightning pitched out of the heavens, spearing the earth somewhere behind the ruined castle. 'Sometimes, my boy, I wonder about you,' he said.

The crash of thunder, the first, José realized, was the harbinger for a sudden powerful gust of wind, and the two men watched as another plastic chair was sent skittering across the patio.

'Don't bother,' José suggested.

'What?' his father asked, surprised at the remark made by his young son.

'I said, don't bother,' José answered. 'You should be wondering about what you did to Enriqueta.'

'José, that's enough. Shut the door and go to bed,' his father ordered.

José turned and watched his father retreating into the shadows. 'This is your doing,' he yelled down the passageway. 'This storm, this strangeness; it's because of you.'

The accusations slammed into the heavy wooden door that Eusebio had closed behind him. Turning to face Mother Nature, José witnessed the first drops of rain and lifted his face to feel the cold wet pearls splash against his skin. With the storm raging about him, he stepped onto the patio, sat on the whitewashed low brick wall and gave thanks to the powers that had sent this inundation to wash away the stain of an imperfect day.

8.   Afternoon

José grumbled as he hauled himself up and into the driver's seat of his recently purchased Toyota.

He grumbled quite a lot these days, especially when having to exert himself, although he had to admit that, sometimes, just listening to María was enough to set him off. God, how the woman could talk! Then there were his legs, both of them, the real ones which were causing him a lot of pain. And he was becoming more impatient, tetchy and less tolerant of those around him. He supposed it was a sign of growing old, but this was something to which he'd *never* admit. And now, he'd forgotten the keys. Damn it to hell, he thought, all of it, everything.

'María!' he yelled. 'Where are my keys?' He grinned stupidly, knowing that María would be throwing silent prayers to the blue yonder and lamenting the fact that her husband was crazy enough to imagine he could drive away without keys. José prodded moodily at the layer of dust coating the dashboard, his stubby forefinger leaving an impression similar in appearance to a moon crater. He was proud of his car and tried to keep it clean, inside and out; it was an uphill struggle, necessitating weekly visits to the carwash at Caleta.

It had taken a while to master the act of feeding coins into the machine without having the spray rod fly around like a wild thing but, once in control, José quite enjoyed the operation. He'd spend ages spraying jets of water at the expanse of metal and glass and, becoming arty, would twist the elongated tube into all the impossible nooks and crannies obligatory to the world of car design, paying particular attention to the array of dead insects that held clam-like to the wiper blades and the radiator grille, lifeless bodies stranded like krill in grinning chrome baleen.

Using his specially purchased chamois leather, he'd dry the vehicle by hand before driving out of the spray booth, thus often becoming the subject of anatomically impossible suggestions yelled by irate jockeys of the tarmac. Unperturbed, cloth in hand, José would stroll around his gleaming steed until the task was complete and then, and only then, drive across the concrete to the monster Hoover that resembled a petrol pump. By this stage he'd be in his element, taking time to remove the foot mats and slap them hard onto the ground before running the extendible suction hose over every inch of seat, shelf, and carpet, and the knobs, dials and switches that he thought gave the compartment the attitude of a flight deck. Finally, he'd replace the rubber mats, wipe the insides of the windows and the rear-view mirror with the damp chamois, and then set off on the homeward journey. Five minutes later, the Toyota would be covered in dust, and the pristine dashboard, already speckled with the first few particles, would be coated in a fine layer by the time the car arrived back at the *cortijo*.

'María!' José yelled again, looking in the rear-view mirror, irritated that she hadn't responded to his first shout.

'Here,' she said, surprising him by standing right alongside the driver's open window.

José turned to look at his wife and found the keys being jangled in front of his face.

'About time,' he said, disgruntled. 'Where were they?'

'On the table, José, where they always are,' she admonished gently and smiled sweetly.

'I'll be back later,' José growled, keying the ignition.

'*Comme toujours*,' María answered, and despite being the sum total of her repertoire of foreign languages, the accent was perfect. She had no idea where she'd picked it up, but the thought of being the only French-speaking person in the district made her distinctly proud. That no one understood this singular phrase, the use of which made her seem a little odd, worried María not in the least.

Still a little uncertain about the amount of pressure to put on the accelerator, José applied too much and the car lurched out of the yard leaving María standing in a cloud of dust.

Whilst manoeuvering the vehicle around numerous pot holes, he started humming to himself, and a couple of minutes later, swinging to the left and heading towards the mountains, recalled where the melody came from.

José imagined he could make out the path he'd followed all those years ago, he and the other escapees; there, up ahead and a little to the right, a faint scratch next to where the pine trees formed a straight vertical line against bare rock. Driving over the humps and bumps of the twisting pitted track, he let his mind wander back to those days of hardship, uncertainty and death. He remembered how it had rained, day after day of torrential rain – Jesus, he could almost feel it – and he remembered the pain in his lungs and the pain in his legs as they'd run . . . run, for God's sake, up the side of a mountain! And the walk through the pine forest, he remembered that too, the silence of carpeted footfalls and the smell of wild herbs crunched underfoot as they made their way across the rugged landscape. And it was then, when they'd eaten their improvised snacks, that they'd sung this song. He was unable to recall the words, but the melody – a marching tune, strong, uplifting, calling the people to stand up and be counted – he'd remember that until the day he died. He started to tap out the rhythm on the steering wheel, *tap-tappitytap-tap-bip-tap-bip-tap*, becoming so engrossed he almost forgot to turn off the track at the point where an overgrown trail led to the smallholding. It's funny, he thought, being able to remember such detail from . . . Christ! sixty years ago, and now I have a problem trying to remember my keys!

He parked alongside Vicente's beaten up Landrover, in the shade of an ancient olive tree, and lowered himself slowly, slowly, until his feet touched the ground. Reaching behind the seat for his stick, José spent a few moments standing still, giving his legs a chance to get used to the idea of doing some work. He leaned against the old Landrover and clucked disparagingly at the state of its interior. Dust, dog hairs, empty beer cans, dust, empty plastic bottles and empty cigarette packets strewn amongst discarded curls of flimsy cellophane; a couple of spanners and a screwdriver, dust, a crate of shrivelled grapes and an oil can lying on its side, the contents leaking out to stain the drifts of thirsty dust. José shook his head as he thought about the fate of the countryside, the remorseless evolution of the dust bowl destined to become an echo of the Red Planet.

The parking place, a patch of worn out earth, was situated close to the water deposit that Vicente had been constructing, and a home-made ladder, propped against the side of the tank, was too much for José to resist. Taking firm hold of the uprights, he launched himself forward to make an inspection of the finished work. One step, then another, faltering and unsteady, pause for breath; then a third and a fourth, and now at last he was high enough to peer over the top of the cylinder. Straightaway, he noticed the concrete beams that Vicente had been discussing earlier in the day. There were five of them, each spanning the circumference of the tank and positioned so as to support the specially lipped blocks slung between them. The segment adjacent to José's vantage point halfway up the ladder, was still uncovered, so he was able to view the cement finish on the interior of the curved wall. He rubbed a finger across the smooth surface and was pleased to find that the finish had been rendered in a fine cement glaze, virtually a watertight skin. Having spent years in the construction industry, including a spell in Switzerland, he knew what he was looking at; indeed, he'd taught Vicente everything he knew.

Muttering 'Bueno, muy bueno,'[38] José slapped his hand against the inside of the tank and listened to the strange ringing sound of the half full container. Survey complete, he descended the rickety ladder, walked back to the 4 x 4 and collected the cool box containing a few bottles of San Miguel he'd taken from the fridge in the garage.

'Hola papa,' Vicente called out, head just visible above a row of tomato plants.

'Hola niño,' José replied, changing direction to walk over to the patch of cultivated ground. He inspected the peppers and the onions and poked his stick amongst the few late lettuces, some of which were well beyond their best. He looked up as Vicente, cigarette dangling from mouth, plastic carrier bag in his hands, wandered round the end of the line of tomatoes and came to stand in front of him.

Vicente held open the bulging bag and displayed a collection of large red fruits. 'Look,' he said, 'I picked these for Mama, and underneath there are some onions.'

José smiled at his son, grunted and placed one of his large hands on the man's shoulder. 'We'll pick 'em up on the way back,' he said, lowering the cool box onto the earth. 'Leave the bag here, next to the beer. Now, where are these pipes?'

'All connected, papa, but there's a problem,' Vicente answered.

'Huh, there's always a problem in the *campo*,' José chuckled as father and son converged on the point where a large black plastic tube disappeared over the edge of the hill. José walked to the top of the steep escarpment and looked down at the network of tubes that Vicente had arranged across the face of the slope. There were three different sizes of tube, the smallest – no thicker than strings of spaghetti – providing the ultimate link between water tank and plant.

'So what's the problem?' he asked, waving his stick in the air. 'It looks fine.'

'The weight of the water and the steep incline,' Vicente explained. 'The water's turned off now, but . . . Jesus, the whole lot nearly ended up at the bottom of the hill.'

The two men peered into distant depths where little was visible save a clump of canes, their slender yellow rods vague etchings in gloomy shadows.

'How?'

'The water, papa. I told you.' Vicente lit another cigarette, exasperation starting to surface. He dragged on the thin unfiltered stick, held the intake in place, then allowed the grey smoke to escape through his nostrils. He turned on his heels. 'Follow me,' he urged.

They walked back towards the water deposit and stopped at a place where there was a break in the large tube. The soil here was much darker and José noticed the fresh earthy smell of damp ground.

'I'll have to repair it,' Vicente said, 'cut and reconnect. The whole thing just pulled itself apart.' He held his hands together, fist against fist, and then separated them, suddenly, demonstrating the parting of the tube. 'I was at the top of the slope, waiting to see the water trickle out of the feeder tubes. It took a while for the network to fill up but as it did, the whole system started to pull away. The weight of the water and the steepness of the slope were too much and by the time I'd run back to turn off the supply, this joint,' Vicente kicked at it, 'had failed. Jesus, it could have been a disaster!'

'It could?' José asked.

'Absolutely it could,' Vicente responded. 'Just think! If I'd left the system running all night and maybe tomorrow as well, the deposit would be empty, the plants would be parched and there'd be a heap of tangled tubing in the gully.'

They spent an hour or so, José and his son, toiling on the steep face of viniculture. Vicente set off down the hillside with a handful of metal stakes, hammering them into the rocky soil at three or four metre intervals alongside the large plastic water pipe. José, in his own time and in his own fashion, followed. They'd found an assortment of odd lengths of cord and string lying around in the back of the Landrover, and

José's job consisted of lashing the tube to the stakes. He was a dab hand at knots, knew them all, from a simple reef knot to a double sheet bend, but today he used a combination of the simplest. He threw a clove hitch around the tube, then, pulling the cord around the nearest stake – once, twice – secured it with a couple of half hitches.

To accomplish the first and second attachments, José had just about managed to bend his ancient body in order to reach the ground, but by the third, he found himself having to kneel. By the time he reached the eighth stake, his knees, sore from being pressed against the uneven stony surface, protested vehemently and José ended up sitting down. But, he was happy, he liked to be involved, it made him feel useful, and before long he was humming that tune again, the tempo occasionally managing to catch up with the regular beat of Vicente's hammer on metal stakes. And then it came to him, the name of the marching melody, "*Cara al Sol*".[39]

Halfway down the hillside the gradient became steeper and José had to scrabble from stake to stake, using feet, hands, and buttocks to prevent a free fall flurry to the bottom. Halfway down the hillside, José stopped humming, having remembered that the song was an anthem beloved and adopted by the Nationalists.

Finally, task accomplished, José and Vicente slowly unfolded their aching limbs. With the palms of their hands pressing into the small of their backs, they stood and looked up at the irrigation system neatly espaliered against the expanse of hill. Satisfied with their labours, they decided against climbing up the almost vertical plantation, electing instead to follow the track, winding backwards and forwards until the hairpins eventually brought them once more to the top of the hill.

While José sat on a small mound of earth and gasped, trying to regain his breath after the unaccustomed exertions, Vicente went to fetch the cool box and the bag of vegetables.

Sitting side by side in the late afternoon, they enjoyed the cold beer and the satisfaction of a job well done, their faces painted red by the huge sun wheeling towards the horizon, red as the tomatoes bunched together in the plastic bag.

'Well, son, shall we go and open the tap?' José suggested.

'No, dad,' Vicente replied. 'I think we've done enough for one day. Let's leave it 'til tomorrow.'

'*Bueno*,' José said in full agreement.

Staring at the point where the earth fell away from sight, he thought about the hundreds of grapevines that would have to wait another day. He thought too about previous years, when winter rains had made it possible to cultivate vines without the necessity of irrigation, although sometimes it had been a close call, very close.

'The world's changing,' he told Vicente, prising the cap from a bottle of beer.

'Yes, papi,' Vicente answered. 'You said that earlier.'

'Maybe, maybe,' José said, his mind trawling through the lunch time conversation and the considered opinion, *his* considered opinion, that nothing would be the same after the horrific attack on democracy and freedom. 'In more ways than one,' he concluded, nodding towards the brow of the hill.

'Yes, papi,' Vicente acknowledged.

'And we need to rescue the frog,' José added, holding out the bottle until it chinked against that in Vicente's hand.

'Frog?' Vicente asked. 'Frog?'

'The beast that called to your mother, after lunch,' José explained.

139

'Beast?' Vicente started to think his father had overexerted himself. 'What beast? What frog?'

'Big seagull? Monster rabbit?' José chuckled. 'Am I helping?'

'Oh, that,' Vicente smiled round the neck of the San Miguel. 'Frog, huh?'

'It's trapped in that old water tank, the one below the almonds; you know, near Manolo's avocados? I couldn't get in to get it out.'

'Poetry, papi, sheer poetry,' Vicente beamed at his father. 'So, you need my help?'

'Yep. Bring a bucket and some string.'

'Sounds like we're going fishing, papi,' Vicenti commented happily.

9. Wedding

The priest was sweating; everybody was sweating. Fingers were inserted into collars and pulled at the heavily starched material, trying to force an aperture large enough to let cool air in, and foetid air out.

José looked at his bride and felt his chest swell with pride. She was the most beautiful woman in the whole of Andalucía. No, he corrected himself, surely she must be the loveliest female in all of Spain. María was radiant, her dark skin and rich black hair contrasting sharply against the brilliant white wedding gown. José's eyes feasted themselves on the low-cut, richly embroidered bodice. Hugging the swell of María's full breasts, the material tapered to her waist where it was cinched tightly so as to exaggerate her young slender figure. Below the waist, the dress swooped in voluminous folds to the large marble tiles that paved the church. Whenever she moved, people finding themselves close enough might have caught a glimpse of tiny satin shoes, each decorated with a crimson bow, peeping out from under the layers of white drapery.

Raising his sight from María's feet, José looked at her face and took in the beauty, the small *retroussé* nose, high cheekbones, generous lips and deep dark-brown eyes. She turned to face him and he noticed the few beads of perspiration that had formed on her upper lip. Lifting his hand, he used his index finger to wipe the moisture from his beloved's face. She smiled, and together they looked around at the assembled multitude, wondering where everybody had come from.

Everywhere, there was movement; ladies waving their fans, flapping them angrily in front of their faces like dark demented butterflies, while the men shuffled uneasily, sporadically dabbing large white handkerchiefs against damp foreheads. Others were making use of the large green-backed hymn books, brandishing them backwards and forwards, causing the pages to rustle like aspens stirring in a breeze.

José wanted to remember every aspect of this momentous day: the people, their clothes; the priest, his clothes; the singing, the church . . .

The church! He looked up at the vaulted ceiling, at the wooden beams and tiny windows set high at the top of the walls. The interior of the church was plain and white, unmarked and unadorned except for a collection of ancient yellowing cords, frayed and greasy, dangling from the heights and used to open and close the windows. Each cord had been decorated with a large crimson bow, fixed at a uniform height about thirty centimetres above the pews. The business end of the church, however, was resplendent, dripping with gold from crucifix to chandelier, chalice to goblet. It was gaudy, tacky, and excessive; Catholic to the extreme with representations of Christs and crosses, saints and sinners, angels, beasts and cherubs, all bedaubed and bedecked with a generosity of sparkling gemstones.

The priest was intoning and incense wafted through the

air; the service seemed to have been in progress forever and José was becoming impatient.

A few days previously, when he and María had visited the tiny church in Daimalos to run through the rehearsal, José had found himself intrigued by some wall paintings that were partially eclipsed by layers of whitewash. Now, as he waited for the priest to stop droning, he allowed his eyes to wander in the direction of the religious frescoes and began to wonder at their history. Who painted them? And why? And when? Then he moved on to the next question. Who covered them up? 'This is ludicrous,' he told himself, 'there's no end to it. Why were they covered? When were they covered? And then someone must have uncovered them again because here they are, large as life.'

José found himself wondering if anyone knew the answers to these deep questions, wondered if anyone would be familiar with the history of the ancient building. Then he seemed to remember being told that the church had been built in the thirteenth century, and while he stood wilting in the presence of God and the population of two villages, José's mind fell into the vacuum of six hundred years. He looked to his right, at Sebastián, his friend from the north whom he'd chosen to be best man. Dressed in his best suit, the man was standing tall and staring straight in front of him, seemingly preoccupied, oblivious to the shufflings and mutterings of the congregation as the priest harped on and on.

A sudden movement above the altar caught José's attention and he noticed a small pink gecko scurrying across the whitewashed wall. He nudged María and nodded in the direction of the lizard, which had started to descend directly towards the altar. José turned to see if anyone else had spotted the intruder, and, sure enough, the eyes of the congregation were fixed on the tiny creature.

The priest, sensing something wasn't quite right, looked up and met the gaze of his audience, only to discover that the attention was focused not on him, but . . . He spun around, his motion frightening the gecko into ungluing itself and plunging, legs and tail akimbo, headlong into one of the goblets ranged along the back of the Lord's Table.

Two seconds later, the reptile's diamond-shaped head reappeared above the rim of the goblet, and in the space of a beady-eyed blink accompanied by ripples of gentle mirth, the creature leapt out of the cup, landed on the reredos, scuttled its way to the top of the banner and promptly disappeared behind the hanging tapestry. The goblet, knocked off balance, teetered and tipped into the next in line and started a domino effect. The result was spectacular. From one end of the altar to the other, everything went flying: golden cups, chalices, candlesticks, and miniature statuettes of Jesus in gold and Jesus in silver. Sliding stealthily out of its hiding place, the gecko pushed its little face over the top of the screen to see what had transpired. The priest, arms outstretched, robes flying, moved hastily towards the scene of desecration, then, changing his mind, returned to his former pose in front of the congregation. Folding his arms across his chest, he paused and took a deep breath. The silence was palpable, and everyone, gecko included, remained rooted to the spot, waiting to see what would happen.

Raising his arms piously to each side, the priest gazed steadfast at his audience. 'And so, in the eyes of the Lord and in the eyes of everyone here present, even in the eyes of the creatures of the world, I pronounce you husband and wife.'

The applause was instantaneous, rapturous and long lasting. José turned to his woman, lifted the veil from her face, and the couple kissed.

'You *may* kiss the bride,' the priest added, smiling at the newlyweds.

Gradually, the tumult decreased and while everybody came forward to shake the hands of the radiant couple, the priest turned his attention to the world of chaos displayed on the surface of the altar.

José was ready to melt. He turned towards his best man and indicated the need for something with which to mop his face. Sebastián, finding himself suddenly necessary, plunged his hands into his pockets and felt his face slide towards the hard church tiles. Disaster.

'The rings!' he cried. 'We forgot the rings!'

The priest, busily trying to organize the holy relics into some sort of order, froze, in something approaching an attitude of benediction. He prayed fervently to his Lord and Master, hoping against hope that some sort of miracle would descend from above, a magic spell that would see the whole congregation, rings in place, moved forthwith and resurrected happy and festive at the reception. He paused, he waited, and not one miracle deigned to attach itself to the resplendent day. The priest was trapped between an obdurate altar and a sea of sweaty expectant people.

'The rings,' he announced, thinking rapidly. 'We will carry out the ceremony of the rings on the church steps, in the light of day, in the full radiance of God's glory.'

Outside, although the heat was more intense under the glare of the blazing sun, a slight breeze whispered across the steps in front of the church and dried the perspiration hanging on the brows of the gathered crowd.

'Who has the rings?' the priest asked the congregation.

'Sebastián has the rings,' the congregation shouted back, amused that the priest should possess such a short memory.

Sebastián, proud as Punch, held the rings aloft, one in each hand between thumb and index finger, and the gathered crowd 'ooh'd' and 'aah'd' at the glittering tokens of betrothal. The priest took the rings from Sebastián and laid them on a small golden cushion, which he'd remembered to bring out of the church with him.

'These rings are the gifts that José and María give to each other as tokens of their love.' He stopped and looked towards the heavens for some inspiration. 'Today,' he continued, 'is a special day. Special, because of this wedding, and . . . special because of the differences. Yes,' he announced, cobbling together the idea that had rushed into his head, 'differences and disturbances. Differences caused by the unusual order of service, and disturbances caused by our little four-legged creature. Because of these differences . . .'

'And disturbances,' came a voice from the crowd.

José scanned the faces arrayed in a semicircle and saw his friend, Viktor, one hand in the air as if asking for permission to speak.

'Yes, Viktor, and disturbances . . .'

'And distances,' Viktor added, a little uncertainly.

'Differences, Viktor, differences,' the priest corrected, smiling pleasantly. 'Because of all these things, we will take them as a sign from the Lord that this wedding shall be a happy one . . .'

'Happy wedding,' the crowd cheered ecstatically.

'And that the marriage, blessed in Heaven and in full sight of God, shall be prosperous and fruitful,' the priest concluded.

'Prosperous and fruitful,' the crowd chanted.

'Fruitifous and prosperful,' Viktor added as a studied afterthought.

The priest gave one of the rings to María, and after she'd placed it onto José's finger and said her vows, the priest gave the other ring to José and the process was repeated.

Everyone was talking, everyone was laughing, and for a while, José and María, although surrounded, found themselves in perfect isolation. María moved her hands up and behind her head and carefully removed the pins that had been holding the veil in place, and her hair, released from pious styling, cascaded expansively down and around her shoulders, flecks of luminosity catching in the brilliant sunshine. She smiled up at her husband and placed an arm about his waist, while her other arm employed itself by raising the discarded veil to mop at her face.

They became aware of people milling about, and the noise of animated chatter, now accompanied by the sound of firecrackers, was overpowering. And here, striding towards them, came María's mother, round, panting, and red of face.

'*¿Qué hacéis? ¡Vamos!*[40] Rocío exclaimed, smiling in a determined sort of manner. She turned and waved her arms, Moses fashion, in the direction of the crowd.

'*¡Venga, venga!* she cried, arms gesticulating wildly. 'Come on! Make way!'

Haltingly, following the orders of the fleshy batons, the crowd shifted backwards to form a human corridor leading from the church steps, down the steep slope and around the

147

corner, to the hamlet's small plaza.

Arm in arm and accompanied by strident strains of fla-
menco vocals, José and María followed Rocío along the chosen
way, each step anointed with handfuls of rice and fragrant
petals. Expanding in much the same way as a rain-swollen
river, the cortège rapidly engulfed the square and began to
flow in eccentric eddies, meeting and greeting late arrivals and
welcoming them into the party.

Dominated by a towering jacaranda, the square was bordered
on one side by a low-level wrought iron fence. Constructed
a few years previously, it was designed to prevent the inhabitants stepping over the edge and damaging themselves on
account of a two metre drop to the mountain track winding
past the village.

Now, plaza, fence, and the immediate surroundings were
unrecognizable. During the forty-five minutes of religious
activities, a small team of venerable ancients had been busily
transforming the place into a multicoloured arena, and the
railing had all but disappeared beneath an assortment of
streamers and flags, and balloons and banners proclaiming
congratulations and messages of luck and long life to the
newlyweds.

The western end of the square backed on to a garage
that served as town hall, community centre, shop and library;
and it was here, against the garage wall, that three or four
trestle tables had been set up, covered in sheets and laden
with alcohol and food. For some unknown reason, the mayor
of a neighbouring metropolis had taken the liberty of install-
ing himself as barman, and together with a couple of elderly
retainers, prowled restively in front of the provisions on dis-

play.

As José and María stepped onto the plaza, a mariachi band let rip with a blistering trumpet fanfare, brilliant and powerful, proclaiming a fortuitous future that thrived for a full ten seconds before sliding to an undignified coda at the behest of the distraught mayor, whose bout of frantic arm-waving caused the musicians to stop playing. The sudden cessation of music caused the assembled multitude to look about, everyone muttering, wondering what had happened; and when the collective focus came to rest upon the mayor, the pockets of suspicious conversation ground to a standstill.

'I have a speech to make,' the mayor announced, puffing up to full pomposity.

'Go on, then,' a voice called from the crowd.

'I have to bless the happy couple,' the mayor continued, louder now, official and more confidant.

'The priest did that,' another voice shouted. Everyone laughed, spontaneous, unrestrained.

'As civic leader, it's my job . . .'

'Get *on* with it,' two or three voices cried in unison.

'. . . my job to start the proceedings,' the mayor completed, looking up in alarm as a large figure loomed in front of him. At the same instant, the band, frustrated and anxious to resume, launched into a complex tango. By the fourth bar, the mayor had been gathered into the arms of a giant and whirled around the square like some rag doll, his movements orchestrated by the muscular arms of Pepe. The wedding guests and villagers stamped their feet and clapped their hands as the unorthodox couple pranced about the makeshift stage, weaving in and out of the onlookers and sometimes crashing into those too slow to move out of the way. Spurred on by the ecstatic crowd, the band increased the tempo, beat by beat, bar by bar, until the music was being played at almost twice its starting speed. Pepe tango'd into a chair and went flying, taking the mayor with him. Rolling to an undignified halt at José's feet, they looked up, startled, and found two bottles of land wine being lowered towards them.

'Drink!' José commanded, passing a bottle to each of the men as they staggered to their feet. 'Drink!'

Hot, giddy, bewildered and thirsty, they drank. It was four-thirty and the party had begun.

Late in the evening, the little village square resembled a battlefield. A handful of hardened revellers, supported by wistful airs from a lone Spanish guitar, swayed majestically in the dimly lit plaza, hands occasionally slapping at an inquisitive mosquito, feet causing empty bottles to spin and skitter across the almost deserted temporary dance floor. A couple of children, a boy and a girl, chased a pair of balloons. In hot pursuit of the troublesome spheres, they crashed into one of the last couples still to be dancing, jumped over a discarded chair and disappeared under the row of tables.

José and María sat and surveyed the scene from the safety of a bench, María sitting more or less upright, José sprawled lengthwise, head resting in his wife's lap; they'd stayed the course. They'd made their speeches, thanked their parents, thanked the priest and one or two other individuals; they'd drunk each others health, they'd danced, they'd sung and they'd cut the cake, and now, exhausted, they didn't know what to do. Most of the guests had gone, leaving in stages during the past hour or so, and María and José, having said goodbye to all of them and having kissed and been kissed by all of them, sat on the edge of transition; the prince and the princess, surrounded by empty bottles, discarded food, tattered and torn decorations, and a family of geckoes snapping contentedly at any mosquito that strayed too close.

María bent forward and kissed her husband on his forehead. 'Come on, my love, it's time to go,' she told him.

José succeeded in raising his head a few inches, but the effort was too much and he dropped back onto the comfortable resting place.

'Come on,' María giggled. 'We can't stay here.'

'I can't move,' José responded. 'I'm done for.'

María helped him lift his head and, with much effort, managed to get him into a sitting position. She stood in front of him and held out her arms, ready to pull her husband to his feet.

'María! Stand aside.' A command, powerful and purposeful.

The deep familiar voice came filtering through the scented night air and a moment later, Pepe was hauling José off the bench. 'Come my friend, you have to sleep,' said Pepe, lifting José onto his shoulders. 'You've a long journey tomorrow.'

Steadying the recumbent body with his left arm, he grabbed one of María's hands and guided her towards a nearby house which had been set aside for the newly married couple.

Pepe entered the lodging and marched across the hallway. Stopping in front of a low wooden door, he swung it open and stood to one side so that María would be the first to enter. The room was small, cool and white, and contained a bed and a chair. The bed head had been decorated with some freshly cut olive branches and, in a niche, perhaps a metre above the bed, a burning oil lamp and a wooden crucifix kept silent vigil. Pepe followed María into the room and turned to close the door.

José, still draped like a sack of potatoes over the man's shoulder, twisted his face away from Pepe's back in an attempt to see what was going on. The world had turned itself upside down and he thought he'd been transported to heaven. He watched an inverted mosquito net being drawn to one side and was amazed to see a bed attached to the ceiling. Open-mouthed, he watched María fold back the bed linen. María? his confused brain asked. What was *she* doing here? He stared at a bed that seemed to be drifting towards him and wondered where his mother was, Inmaculada, the woman who prepared his meals, bathed his cuts and bruises and who, for most of his existence, put him to bed. Stretching his hands upwards, he felt the coolness of the sheets and marvelled at the pillow descending towards his heavy head, embracing, soothing, comforting. José's fatigue disintegrated and found sanctuary in soft oblivion.

The light was painful, excruciatingly painful. Raging against fluttering eyelids, remorselessly it dragged José through layers of unconsciousness. It was like diving into an ocean, the one that was hovering above his head, scintillating and full of green light. No, wait, now it was blue; yes, blue light, bright blue light. *Joder*, it was like the light from a thousand diamonds, a million candles, and it was burning away the clouds, the huge white fluffy clouds that filled José's head. And then something happened.

He opened his eyes and the world was white; it was too white, so he shut his eyes for a few seconds before opening them again, this time no wider than a slit. Rubbing a hand across his face, he listened to the sound of stubble, loud in the sea of white tranquillity. He opened his mouth and tasted the stale breath lingering behind his teeth and under his tongue. *Mierda*. José cranked his eyelids a little wider and squinted across the room. He saw María looking down at him, saw her beautiful radiant smile, and then he noticed her hands; they were holding something.

She was sitting next to him on the bed and on her lap was a plateful of fruit – grapes, peaches, mangoes. José wondered where the peaches and mangoes had come from, but didn't let it bother him for long, he was hungry, ravenous, thirsty also. María's hands brought a peach to his mouth.

After a while, she used a cloth to wipe the juice from her husband's chin and to dab beguilingly at the corners of her own mouth. 'There's a surprise,' she told him, smiling.

'Surprise?' José asked in a sleepy voice.

'Yes, outside. Come on,' she said, laughing and throwing his clothes at him.

José stumbled out of bed and pulled on the clothes, fresh clothes which had been resting on the chair all night, waiting, patient and unnoticed.

'Come *on!*' María called exuberantly, unable to contain her excitement. She moved to the door and opened it and stepped out into the hall, then stepped back into the room. She was a little girl, young and uncertain, wanting to be everywhere at the same time.

'José! Hurry up!'

Together, they emerged into sunshine and shyly looked about, their eyes adjusting gradually to the glaring noonday light.

Small groups of well-wishers stood chatting to one another, but fell silent when they saw José and María. Then, with one accord, they swarmed round the newlyweds and led them across the plaza towards the solitary jacaranda. There, gleaming richly beneath a filigree of green leaves, purple-blue flowers and small wrinkled brown sachets dangling like dried-up scrotums, stood a surrey, its ebony framework polished to a mirror-finish.

Exhorted by their friends, María and José climbed on board and in the manner of royalty, took up position on the rear seat. Eagerly inspecting the quaint form of transport, they feasted their eyes on the brass lamps, one at each corner, the garlands of flowers attached to every available surface, and the long strips of multicoloured ribbon draping to the ground behind them.

The driver cracked his whip and the entourage set forth, negotiating slowly the steep cobbles leading down and out of the village.

María, believing she was a real princess, behaved in regal fashion, waving at the people she was leaving behind and smiling at everything; she was euphoric, she had her man and nothing could go wrong.

José, despite a certain queasiness, felt the same, and from time to time he too ventured a wave at the spectators, their numbers thinning as the carriage, beginning to pick up speed, drew away from the small hamlet. Placing an arm around María's shoulders, he pointed ahead at the two greys, mares, dressed in all their finery. Resplendent against the horses' coats, the harnesses, belts and buckles seemed to be alive, vibrant with the easy movement of the powerful muscles they embraced.

With ribbons rippling in the breeze, the surrey continued its downhill journey until a bend in the track hid it from view. One by one, the villagers, friends and relations, stopped waving and the small crowd began to disperse, drifting through sunlight and shadows to their homes. The little square, held in place by its wrought iron fence and presided over by the towering jacaranda, was deserted.

10. Interlude

A light breeze caressed the back of José's neck, causing him to smile. Idly, he raised his hand, lifted it to his head and ran his fingers through his hair. Shit, he thought, where's all my hair gone? He was prevented from thinking any further by the touch of something else brushing against his neck. Hell, what could this be? It was firm yet gentle, and felt vaguely like a horse's tail.

'That'll be what it is,' he muttered to himself. 'It'll be one of the mares. Darned animal's got too close.'

And there it was again, the same sensation of something brushing at the back of his neck. He moved his hand to slap at the offending tail and then it dawned on him that it couldn't be a tail. 'No,' he said, grappling with reality, 'it's impossible. The horses are meant to be in front.'

'Horses? What horses?' María asked, removing the paint-brush from her husband's neck. 'Unless of course it was horses that dragged you away, you know, stopped you from helping with the whitewash?'

'We just got married,' José informed her, his mind gallop-ing through fifty years, returning him swiftly to the here and now. 'We were in a horse and cart.'

'We were,' María agreed, unfazed, showing him the paint-brush. 'Look, new and unused.'

Well attuned to such jibes, José ignored it and leaned forward to smack a fly that was investigating his beer.

'What are those Arabs doing, then?' he asked, trying to focus on the television that had been attempting to impart the selfsame information.

'I wouldn't know,' María answered, plonking a half-full tub of paint onto the stained stone slab under the tap. 'Some of us are too busy . . .' The rest of the sentence was lost, drowned by the sound of running water.

'Stupid woman,' José grumbled. 'Always trying to compete against noise.'

He turned his head to catch sight of her stumping around the corner of the cottage, straining to carry the now heavy tub of diluted paint. He sighed and picked up the beer, took a sip and grimaced as warm lager swirled down his throat. 'Bollocks,' he said, replacing the can and misjudging the top of the table. Crashing with a thud into the unyielding surface, two or three dollops of beer leapt out of the can and landed on his hand. 'Bollocks,' he said again, wiping his hand on a trouser leg. He grunted, levered himself out of the chair and tried to stand upright, the muscles in his back stretching in painful protest at the abuse sustained during the staking out of the irrigation system. He grabbed his stick and lumbered off in the direction taken by María.

José was always amazed at the amount of work that María seemed able to cram into the space of one day. He had no idea how she managed to do it. Somewhere, he'd heard a strange rumour about work schedules in these warmer climes, about how men supposedly were quite content to sit back and put the world to rights, while the women got on with the work. It was gossip he didn't spend too much time worrying about, and anyway, if women wanted to work all the hours God gave them, who was he to stop them?

He rounded the corner and gazed at the newly white-washed wall, shiny and bright in early evening sunlight. He leaned back and placed his hands on his hips, fingers splayed out across the small of his back. Looking up and down and from side to side, he was unable to find a single missed spot on the uneven pebble dash surface.

A sudden movement caught his attention and he craned his head to witness María's left hand holding a small can of paint. From where he was standing that was all he could see, so he stepped back a couple of paces until he was able to watch María as she toiled away at maintaining the house. José stood rooted to the ground, transfixed, full of admiration for this woman, his wife, the only woman he'd loved. This was by no means the first time he'd observed María at work but, nonetheless, he was impressed and his heart went out to her.

'It's not too late, you know,' María called out without raising her line of sight from the busy paintbrush. 'I can easily fill another can with paint.'

José shuffled over and stood behind her, placing his hands onto her shoulders. 'I really don't think you need any help from me,' he told her, bending forward to kiss the top of her head. 'You're the expert.'

He turned away, hesitantly, and walked slowly alongside the freshly painted wall until he came to the kitchen. Collecting a cold beer from the fridge, he returned to his domain in front of the television and glowered at the screen and a commercial eulogizing the benefits of owning a mobile phone. Grunting at slick advertising, José ripped the tab from the can, took a couple of gulps in quick succession and carefully placed the container onto the table. Glancing at the tabletop, he happened to notice his phone lying face down an inch or two from where he'd put the can. He picked it up and turned it over; no messages and no missed calls.

José was in two minds about this new vogue, these small portable things that seemed to be everywhere. He didn't really like them, thought they were too intrusive. He remembered joking with his friends in the village. 'Bloody things,' he'd said. 'It's like having a receiver built into the end of your arm, who needs it?'

He recalled that someone had replied that they were useful for emergencies, for calling the doctor if you had an accident while working in the shed. Someone else had told the story of how he'd used his mobile phone to call his wife, telling her he'd be home late and that he was in an important meeting at the *ayuntamiento*, while his other hand had been holding the beer bought for him by his friends in the pub.

José had pondered long and hard on this, and on reflection had decided that perhaps they were quite useful after all. He was happy anyway that his son had a mobile with him at all times. It gave him some peace of mind knowing that Vicente could contact him at anytime, should he, God forbid, have some mishap while working in the *campo*. Then he remembered the few frustrating occasions when he'd tried to get in touch with Vicente, but had been unable to do so because there had been no signal.

'Bloody things,' he muttered into the beer glass. 'Bloody useless modern contraptions.'

160

Using his stick to intimidate a plastic chair into position in front of him, he raised his feet onto it and folded his mind in upon itself. José was a great thinker and every day he'd spend a good deal of time, legs stretched out, pondering life and all its intricacies. Within a few minutes he'd be snoring, mouth open, head lolling uncomfortably against the stained material of the armchair and then, mid snore, he'd wake up, snap shut his mouth, look furtive, feel guilty, and go back to sleep.

The sun, unnoticed, followed its sedate migration towards winter solstice and its turning point between the Pillars of Hercules. And as shadows lengthened and the evening chorus of swallows, cicadas and whining mosquitoes built towards shrill discord, the dogs became restive and José's comatose imagination blossomed into the logic of lateral thinking.

Shit! he gasped, it was so easy. Three in one and one in three! He must have been dreaming about it, subconscious elements clicking away like some monstrous computer.

Surprised by the revelation, José leaned forward and his feet slid off the chair, knocking it into a dusk-filled corner. Groping across the tabletop, he located his mobile phone and pressed its button to wake it up. Bright green figures gleamed out of his palm, 7:51. His eyes, adjusting themselves to the small rectangle of light, quickly had to readjust when time ceased to exist.

Damn, now he couldn't recall what it was it he'd been thinking about. Christ, he thought, my memory's leaking like . . . Christ! that's it, God! He said the word aloud, 'God', to be sure he'd latched on to the correct memory. Some-where close at hand, María was doing something with water, sloshing something about in a bucket. The noise infiltrated José's reasoning and his moment of precious inspiration was gone, drowned. And then the noise stopped, and in deafening silence José's imagination saw God the Father, God the Son and God the Holy Ghost, standing defiant under a giant wave.

'He made us in his own image,' José shouted across the patio.

'*Hombre*,' María responded. 'I'm going to feed them now, when I've put the paint stuff away.'

'God,' José mumbled, rubbing at his eyes and wondering why he'd woken up all religious, wondering why his wife was being so obtuse. 'Who?' he asked her, thinking that perhaps he *hadn't* woken up.

'Nearly finished,' María told him, ignoring the question, 'just a few more awkward places. There's one more wall to go but I'll get it done tomorrow, when you and Vicente rescue the frog.'

José forgot the question and scratched at an irritation behind his right knee. Shifting himself upwards in the chair, he tried to assemble his scattered thoughts. Must be all the death, destruction and uncertainty, he reasoned, as the images, *those* images, escaped from the screen and fled into gathering darkness. He yawned and attached his mind to the celestial Omnipotence, the concept that floated about like a lump of familiar furniture, something that existed but didn't warrant attention. He wasn't religious, not at all, and very seldom gave the matter thought, but now, now that he had it by the balls, he wasn't going to let go.

'I'm God,' he informed his wife.

'Yes dear,' María agreed.

'You as well,' he told her.

'I'll get you something to eat,' María suggested, calm, efficient, knowing, 'after I've attended to the birds.'

'Ah, birds,' José announced, sudden revelation burning beacon-like, supplying the answer to his circumvented question. 'Birds.'

'What about them?' María asked, shuffling round the corner with her hands full of paintbrushes and dirty rags.

'You're going to feed them; *them*,' José answered intelligently.

'Yes dear, I told you.' María placed her hands on her hips and let out a long troubled breath. 'Sometimes . . .'

'Anyway,' José interrupted, returning to matters profound. 'I'm God, you're God, we're all God,' he insisted. 'All of us, God.'

'All of us?' María asked doubtfully.

'You, me, Vicente . . . Jaime; all of us, everybody,' José answered.

María stood still and pondered the matter. 'Sebastián?' she asked, cautiously.

'Yep.'

'Viktor?'

'Yep.'

María turned to enter the *cotijo*, paused, and over her shoulder asked, 'Mother?'

'Everyone, María, everyone. Sebastián, Viktor, Rocío . . . Banderas . . . Aznar . . .'

'Banderas?' María's voice queried from the dark interior. 'Are you sure?'

'You see? He made us in his image,' José called back, edging carefully around the problem, testing, probing, groping through the valley of difficult things.

'Banderas the God,' María stated, as though recalling the

title of a film.

'Not the God, María; not *the* God, but *a* God,' José said, eyeing the plate that María placed on the table. 'I'm a God, you're a God. Like I said, we're all Gods,' he announced triumphantly.

'*Hombre*, where do you get these ideas?' María asked, shaking her head.

José looked up at his wife's round face. 'Don't know,' he replied, 'they just . . . come.' He picked his nose and waited while María completed another circuit into and out of the kitchen. 'That's what so fantastic,' he said to the returning footsteps, 'you just don't know. You could be born a good person or you could be born a bad one.'

'What's so good about that?' María asked.

'Well,' José answered, waking up to the fact that food had appeared on the table and beginning to wonder why he'd launched into this conversation. 'It's up to the individual, we have to make the best of ourselves. All of us, each of us.'

'Don't we do that anyway?'

'Yes, *we* do, but there are those who don't,' José replied.

'Who?'

Now it was getting complex. 'Oh, you know,' José said vaguely, not wanting to dig any further into his pit of confusion.

'Who?' María repeated, settling herself down.

'The people who did that, for a start,' José answered, gesturing at the television set.

'Oh,' said María, calmly splitting a gherkin. 'I thought you were talking about local people.'

'I was talking about everyone,' José retorted. 'We're all the same, all equal . . . only some aren't.'

164

Later, slouched in his chair, José tried to focus on the flickering screen and another commercial, sponsored by the *Junta de Andalucía*,[41] which was busily promoting the wonders of southern Spain. He watched as pictures of weather-eroded rocks juxtaposed with flamenco-singing gypsies; he yawned as lakes and forests blended magically into sun-drenched beaches; and when Arabic palaces began crumbling into enormous dishes of paella, José decided it was time to sleep and disengage his id.

11. *Semana Santa*

Sunlight danced on a gentle sea as the bus chugged along the coast road towards Málaga. The coach was bursting with humanity – everyone had wanted to be included on this trip to the yearly festivities held in the big city – and, to help ease the congestion, José found himself squeezed tightly against a window, Jaime and Raquel keeping him wedged in secure immobility. The threesome, struggling to remain seated on just two seats as the bus thrummed through the narrow quarters of El Palo, struggled also to contain their excitement.

Easter had arrived early this year and the weather was seasonally unsettled. Head and shoulders fleeced in a skimpy mantle of fresh snow, La Maroma, having risen a few geological minutes ago from beneath the sea, sat massively, brooding protectively above the huddled foothills. The sparse collection of villages and hamlets, clinging with obstinate determination to these lofty realms, were visited almost daily by chill breezes seemingly from all points of the compass. Rumour had it that the coastal region offered a few more degrees of warmth, but the crowd, packed into the spluttering bus, took no chances; rumours were rumours and not to be trusted.

Over their shirts, sweaters and jackets – smart shirts, smart sweaters devoid of holes, and their best Sunday jackets – they wore thick winter coats. The villagers had wanted to appear immaculate on this, the most important outing of the year.

*　　*　　*

'What's Málaga like?' Aurelio had been heard to ask the night before.

The noise in the compact pub slithered to a hushed silence and the regulars looked at one another, confusion on their faces, uncertainty in their minds.

'Don't know,' José replied, placing his half-empty glass of beer on the well-worn wooden bar, thinking simultaneously that it was time he started to head towards home.

'Never been,' said Carlos, which for him was unusual, as out of the eleven or twelve people who gathered every evening at the same place at the same time, Carlos was the most widely travelled. Such was his claim and there had never been any reason to doubt him – until now. He was the acknowledged village authority on the geography of Andalucía, Spain, and probably the world; and his peers, having ventured no further than the extent of their vision, cropped and bordered by the tracks of the *campo*, had absolute faith in his perceived wisdom.

'But Carlos, you've been everywhere! That's why we call you Marco Polo,' Aurelio reminded him in an awkward sort of way.

'I know,' Carlos agreed, a heady mixture of alcohol and sudden embarrassment turning his tanned cheeks the colour of ripe plums. 'Everywhere, but not Málaga.'

'It's big,' a gruff voice informed them from the vicinity of the door.

Eleven or twelve pairs of eyes swivelled to focus on the rugged outline stepping into the tiny parlour.

'Pepe!' eleven or twelve mouths voiced in unison.

Pepe, a shepherd, was the hero of the village. Tall, swarthy and darkly handsome, he was the idol of the entire female population and the envy of most of the menfolk. He'd carved a name for himself when he'd rescued a village lad who'd been thrown from a horse. The poor unfortunate, crashing into rocks and olive trees as he'd rolled thirty metres down a steep bank, had ended up with his broken body hidden, half-buried beneath one of the treacherous *chumbo*[42] cactus plants.

He'd been discovered the following day and it had been Pepe who'd found him. The shepherd had picked him up and carried him all the way to the village, whereupon, with the assistance of old Pilar, the respected lady of medicine, he'd re-set the broken leg and the broken wrist and, painstakingly, had removed the vicious spines protruding porcupine-like from the boy's limp body.

'Pepe, have you been to Málaga?' he was asked in hushed tones.

No one could imagine travelling such a distance – Vélez-Málaga was the centre of the universe. Sometimes though, the ancients would tell stories of people who'd journeyed all the way to Granada, and further, on foot! Not so long ago, either. The gnarled regulars knew well the value of their tales, and fuelled with proffered libations of beer and Ponche,[43] happily embellished the legends of gruelling treks to distant lands. They spoke of ancestors, tough *hombres*[44] who'd travelled deep into the interior, herding sheep and goats and pacing endless kilometres behind mules laden with baskets of salted fish.

'No.' The answer was short and simple.

'But how . . .'

'I've been to El Palo,' Pepe explained, full of pride.

'El Palo?' Carlos asked. 'What's El Palo?'

'It's a place on the coast, just a little bit this side of Málaga.'

'And what were you doing, Pepe, to be just a little bit this side of Málaga?' José chided his friend.

'Fishing,' Pepe replied, grinning widely.

'Fishing,' everyone echoed, nodding sagely.

José, however, wasn't convinced. 'It's a long way just to go fishing,' he pointed out, thinking of a ramshackle fishing village a stone's throw from Vélez. 'What's the matter with Mesquetilla?'

'Nothing, so far as I know,' Pepe answered. 'Anyway, who's going to buy me a drink?'

'Come on, then,' José said, 'I'll buy you a drink. But first, you must tell us how come you happened to be fishing in El Palo.'

'Well, I was with my father and his friend Rafael . . .'

'I know Rafael,' said a voice from the bar. 'He's got a boat.'

'Yes, Rafael's got a boat,' Pepe acknowledged. 'And it was from his boat that we were fishing. We'd spent an hour or so hauling lobster pots and were about to turn back, when Rafael thought it would be a good idea to stream some lines for mackerel. The sea was starting to become a little choppy . . . apparently that's when you fish for mackerel.'

'What's this got to do with Málaga?' Carlos asked.

'*Joder*, Carlos,' José complained. 'Let the man continue. It's a good story, good enough to earn him his beer.'

'Anyway,' Pepe resumed, looking sternly at Carlos. 'We were taking it in turns to row into the breeze, which was steadily growing stronger and stronger.'

'Stronger and stronger,' a voice echoed, repeating the words slowly, stretching them to give maximum emphasis.

'Viktor, *¡cállete!*' everyone yelled.

It was okay to tell Viktor to 'shut up', he accepted it in good faith; he knew they were all laughing at him but they were his friends, his peers, his family. They'd grown up together, been to school together, and they'd run wildly around the countryside throwing olives and almonds at one another. That's when Viktor had run straight into a tree. He hadn't been the same since.

Carlos moved across to where Viktor was standing, slapped him on the back and signalled for the barman to fill Viktor's glass.

Attention returned to Pepe, who'd taken the opportunity to sit on the stool that Carlos had vacated.

'So, the sea became rougher and rougher and . . .'

'Rougher and rougher,' Viktor repeated, quietly this time, barely more than a whisper.

'Until Rafael decided he'd had enough. Well, we looked around and didn't know where we were. The current had taken hold of the boat and we'd drifted a long way from the mark. Luckily, we weren't too far out, otherwise we'd have been sunk.'

'Sunk,' Viktor agreed, slurping at his beer.

'We headed towards the shore and it took an hour, an hour of heavy rowing through huge waves.'

Everyone looked at Viktor to see if he had anything to say, but it seemed he was too busy enjoying his drink.

'El Palo, that's where we landed,' Pepe concluded.

*   *   *

Because of the heady influx of people, the city centre had been closed to traffic and the bus was therefore unable to venture further than the bullring. Pushed from behind by the expectant visitors from the *campo,* José and his family were squeezed out of the vehicle and followed the crowds in the general direction of old "one-arm", the cathedral with its single tower peeping above the palms lining the wide swathe of the Paseo del Parque.[45] High above, to the right, the crenellated walls of the Alcazaba ascended in russet-brown ranks towards Gibralfaro Castle, the lofty Arab structure dominating the surrounding area.

José couldn't believe he was here; he'd seen pictures, of course, but actually to be standing here, poised at the entrance to this enormous magnificent city, was momentous. The streets, full of noise and bustle, were crowded with vendors making the most of this week of religious festival; just like the *feria* in Vélez-Málaga, only ten, twenty, a hundred times bigger. The sights were similar, the smells also: almonds roasted in olive oil and sprinkled with salt, candy bars and popcorn, wine, beer and tobacco; and although only ten o'clock and relatively cool, hanging over everything was the intrinsic pervasive odour of soap and sweat.

From somewhere up ahead came the sound of music, the heavy thump of a bass drum accompanied now and then by a cacophony of shrill bugles. The crowd, surging forward in an endeavour to see what was going on, gave the family no option but to follow. Jaime, finding a bench to stand on, quickly hauled his young brother up into the air to stand alongside him. Standing on tiptoe, José was able to see the band, a military band, and soldiers all dressed in green, all marching very rapidly with rifles sloped across their shoulders. The brothers had never experienced such a spectacle – the precise swinging of arms and legs, the heavy crunch of marching boots – and feasted their eyes, squinting at the dazzling reflections burning on a forest of fixed bayonets. And all too soon it was over; the polished leather boots wheeled themselves around a corner and the undisciplined hordes melted back onto the broad *Paseo*. José looked at the crowd squeezing around the bench and scanned the sea of unfamiliar faces. Unable to see his parents and feeling a nudge of anxiety, he pulled at his brother.

'We've lost them, Jaime,' he said. 'Or they've lost us.'

'Don't worry,' Jaime replied, unconcerned.

'But we'll never find them amongst this lot,' José complained, eyes roving wildly across the bustle of humanity. 'Look! Just look!' he cried, waving his arms and sort of flapping them. 'I've never seen so many people.' He twisted round to see Jaime scanning the multitudes, hand held above his eyes so he could see against the glare of the sun. 'Well?'

'Over there, José,' Jaime pointed. 'Over by that lamppost.'

'So let's go,' José yelled, leaping from the bench, only to find himself being grabbed and swung back into place beside his brother. 'Come on,' he shouted, pulling, struggling. 'Let's go, let's go.'

'José, stop wriggling,' Jaime ordered. 'By the time we get there, they'll have been swept away, further along the *Paseo*.'

'But . . .'

'We arranged a meeting place,' Jaime explained to the worried youngster.

'When? Where?'

173

'The cathedral steps,' Jaime informed his brother. 'Two o'clock.'

'Two o'clock?' José asked. 'Two o'clock? That's ages.'

'So let's go and see the harbour. Look, we're not too far from the lighthouse.'

José spun around and from his vantage point above the bobbing heads, was able to see a stubby building in the distance.

'But . . .'

'Come on,' Jaime challenged, jumping to the ground. 'I'll race you.'

'Where have you *been*?' Eusebio scowled, red-faced and impatient, arms held out to his sides in a gesture of dismay. 'Where have you been?' In exasperation, he clouted Jaime over the head. José smirked.

'Well?' Eusebio demanded.

'Calm down, papa,' Jaime said.

'*Calm* down? *Calm* down? Do you know what time it is?' Eusebio asked the boys.

Jaime looked up at the tower looming over them. 'Half-past two,' he answered.

José sniggered.

'José, shut up,' Eusebio fumed. 'Yes, precisely. Half-past two. Can't you tell the time?'

'But . . . I just did, papa,' Jaime replied, then thought he'd emphasize the point. 'I just did.'

'Two-thirty, papa,' José chimed in, supporting his brother.

'José! Shut *up!*' Eusebio yelled. He batted Jaime over the head, again. '*Now* you tell the time, *both* of you. What's the matter with you?' he asked, eyeing first one then the other.

'Nothing,' they replied in tandem.

'Well then,' Eusebio said, uncertain how to conclude the episode.

'It's Holy Week, papa,' José said. 'Everybody's s'posed to be peaceful . . . and nice.'

'You two stop looning around and I'll *be* peaceful and nice,' Eusebio said, turning on his heels. 'Follow me.'

It was an order, not to be trifled with, and gave no room for crafty manoeuvres. Glancing at one another, the brothers fell into step behind their father.

'And stop *snigg*ering,' Eusebio threw over sagging shoulders.

Staying close on Eusebio's heels, they plunged into deep shadows that hung suspended in intriguing alleys. Eusebio seemed to be on a mission; left right left right they went, mimicking the troops; left right left right they went, ever further into the cool interior of the labyrinth.

Suddenly, Eusebio disappeared into a doorway and the boys almost fell over themselves as they skidded to a halt, sorted themselves out and followed their father into the smoky atmosphere.

'Hello boys.' Inmaculada's voice floated out of murkiness. 'Your father found you, then?'

'Yes, Inma, eventually they decided to turn up,' Eusebio answered, struggling through a narrow gap between two tables. 'Kind of them, don't you think?'

'Raquel!' Jaime exclaimed, noticing the slim girl sitting next to his mother. 'Where have you come from?'

'Over there,' she answered, nodding towards an adjacent table.

José, who was finding the whole sequence of events hilarious, spluttered with laughter when he discovered Raquel's family sitting next to him in the gloom.

'They're here, they're there, they're everywhere,' he announced through a wide-mouthed grin.

'Who are?' Jaime asked.

'They are, we are,' José answered intellectually

'We?'

'Me, and you, and you and me, and Raquel; and that makes three,' José trilled, swiftly becoming the centre of attention and then regretting it as he felt the daggers from startled eyes.

'José!' Eusebio began, only to be interrupted by an enormous dish of paella, steaming and fishy.

The vision sent José, open mouthed and giggling foolishly, on a mind trip to the feeding of the five thousand and back. Platefuls of bread arrived and José's stomach reached out, persuading him to pick up a deft chunk and dip it into the soggy mess of rice. Hunger, that was his problem, exacerbated by the excitement of the day, the admonishments from his father, and the distance between here and breakfast. They were still watching, the mournful staring eyes, watching and waiting for José to become unstuck. But not Raquel's, hers were smiling, laughing, adrift with happy encouragement. José stared across the stranded clams and willed her to come and sit next to him and then his mother's arm moved from his left eye into his right and a ladleful of paella slopped onto his plate. Raquel, oblivious to the best advances of José's silent wishes, didn't move.

'José, eat.' His mother's voice leapt into his ear, colliding with his anvil.

He stabbed another wedge of bread into the congealed heap of long-whiskered prawn heads and crayfish tails and wondered about the world in general, why it was the way it was and what it must be like to be an adult.

After lunch, the two families, strolling through the mystifying maze of alleys north of the cathedral, chanced upon a ragged army of believers struggling to haul their Virgin through the confines of Plaza de Campos. Young José pleaded with his father to lift him onto his shoulders – pleading that earned him a clip across the head and left him, ears burning and eyes smarting, with no option but to push his way to the front of the crowd.

The scene, sweatily-staged among piercing shafts of swirling sunlight, was pure carnival: bells rang, people sang, and those who couldn't, yelled and clapped their hands as the heavy burden swayed remorselessly, pace by weary annual pace, towards its destiny. José of the two families was snatched out of his deliberations and found himself being escorted through the crowds, his parents and Jaime – who'd carried out the snatching process – and Raquel and her parents, marching steadfastly towards Plaza de le Merced, where they stationed themselves next to the cenotaph of General Torrijos.

'Are we going home now?' José asked his brother.

'No, José, we're not,' his father answered. 'It's your mother.'

'My mother? What's my mother?' José turned to Inmaculada for enlightenment. 'Mama?'

'It's my feet, José,' she told him painfully. 'And my legs.'

José thought his brain was going to melt and stared at his brother. Thinking it might help the situation, he raised his forearms out to the side, palms forward, and asked '¿Y?' [46]

'We can't go home, José,' his brother explained. 'Not until

the bus comes to collect us.'

'¿*Y?* José repeated, wondering what could possibly be the matter with everyone.

Raquel came to the rescue, an Elysian goddess leaning forward to rest her lips, her beautiful soft lips, against José's ear. 'So you're coming with me and Jaime.'

'Where are we going?'

'Adventure, José,' Raquel explained. 'We're going to explore.'

'What? Where?'

'Never mind what, never mind where, we're just going to go walkabout,' Raquel said through a winning smile.

'Let's go, then!' José called out. '¡*Vamos!*'

'Just a minute,' Jaime said, catching hold of José's arm. 'Look, here comes that Virgin!'

With one accord, the two families looked in the direction indicated and watched the procession wind itself unsteadily around the corners of the small sunlit square.

*   *   *

The youngsters wandered through the narrow quarters bordering the river. They walked tall, invincible, proud to be wearing their best clothes, their swaggering gait aided by the beer and *tapas* they'd just consumed in a small dingy bar. Raquel walked along between the two brothers, her arms around their waists, her hips swaying from side to side in a movement accentuated by a long dress which flounced enticingly with each and every step.

José loved his mother and father, loved them to the moon and back, but Jaime and Raquel . . . they were different, Raquel especially; he'd been in love with her ever since clapping eyes on her at the *feria*. They were young and they knew how to have fun, and they laughed all the time, and . . . and just this morning Jaime had raced him to the lighthouse and bought him a glass of Ponche. A flash of inspiration landed somewhere between José's eyes and crawled into his awareness, and he came to understand his freedom, his unrestrained uniqueness and the strangeness that had consumed him at lunchtime.

Deliriously happy, José glided through the city as if on a cushion of air. For several long hours, the streets of Málaga were his – no parental overtones and no restrictions. The alleys and courtyards, teeming with people and cluttered with churches, shops, markets, bars and bodegas, were fantasies unbelievably real. He squeezed his vision into altered dimensions, living and breathing the sights and sounds of the ancient Phoenician town.

Above him, a thin slice of indigo sky seemed to be all that separated the ridiculously tall buildings, a tenuous force that kept them from crashing into the pastel-coloured canyons of bricks, tiles, balconies, fancy wrought iron and heavy wooden shutters. He wondered about the people who lived in such places; what would they do all day with no vines to prune and no olives to harvest? He couldn't imagine waking up in the morning and looking out of the window, as these people undoubtedly did, at a mirror image of your own apartment. He reckoned it would drive him crazy – no trees, no hills or mountains, and no animals. Still, with all the noise and the hustle and bustle of everyday commerce, he supposed it must be exciting. Just like today, he told himself, and then remembered that today was special. José wasn't too sure about the religious side of things and from the way everyone was acting, got the impression that he wasn't alone in his uncertainty. He felt a little uneasy about the fact that he never went to church, didn't even attend Sunday school, and yet here he was, caught up in a five-hundred-year-old bun fight.

With no real objective, they were content to stroll in any direction their feet led them and a few minutes later, found themselves ambling vaguely towards Plaza de Puerta Nueva. Coming across a sizable gathering of people, they decided to stop for a while and see what was going on. The crowd, a mixture of all ages, was huddled in small groups, everyone talking and laughing but in a subdued sort of way. José found himself standing next to an elderly woman, short and stout, her ample bosom protected with a shawl of fine lace, black, tinged with white.

'*Señora*,' he said, '*buenas tardes. ¿Perdona me, pero qué pasa aquí?*[47]

'This is the home of the Virgen de Puerta Nueva,' the lady replied, pointing to a pair of giant portals attached to a building hidden in a corner of the plaza. 'They'll be bringing her out soon.'

José thanked the woman profusely, almost genuflecting in his desire to show respect for the aged person. He moved across the small square and caught up with Jaime and Raquel, both of whom were staring at a girl dressed from neck to foot in a long flowing red cape. In the girl's hands was one of the tall pointed hats about which José had heard so much gossip. Now, here he was, face to face with the real thing. The girl was chatting animatedly with a young man dressed in a military uniform – probably her boyfriend, José surmised, before realizing it could equally well be the girl's father, or brother; he had no idea and wheeling around to stand behind Jaime, felt slightly foolish at thinking along such ridiculous lines.

He stood on tiptoe and peered over Jaime's shoulder, watching as the girl turned and glanced up at the man standing beside her. She smiled, and José gazed across the square at the most beautiful face he'd ever seen. Somewhere far above his head, the opening or closing of a window caused a stray beam of sunlight to slant down and illuminate perfectly the goddess clothed in red. Once again, powerful sensations scratched at José's groin. He lowered his head and in order to suppress a squeal of passion, clamped his teeth firmly into Jaime's shoulder.

'*¡Joder!* José, what the fuck are you doing?' Jaime yelped.

José, eyes wide with embarrassment, relinquished his toothy grip and muttered, '*Nada, no hago nada.*'

Raquel looked at Jaime's young brother and saw the concern on his face.

'*Mira,*[48] Jaime, your brother's blushing!' she exclaimed with delight. 'Oh, I think he must be in love.'

'Me? In love?' José protested. 'No, never,' he responded, stamping a foot in annoyance as he answered his own question.

Jaime turned to face his brother, the movement opening a channel of vision between the girl in red and the crimson-faced José. For a precious moment their eyes met, two lines of intense communication, and then, as the enormous doors of the *cofrada*[49] began to open, the crowd shifted and the rarefied contact was lost.

Suddenly, the square became a hive of activity – someone was ringing a hand-bell and a wave of people, all clutching pointy red hats, began separating themselves from the masses.

Caught on the periphery, José, Jaime and Raquel were shuffled backwards and forwards, this way and that, like ducks at the mercy of raging waters.

Unable to see what was going on, José began to pester his companions. '*¿Qué pasa?*' he cried. '*¿Qué pasa?*'

'*Nada, José. Nada,*' Raquel answered.

'But there's so much noise, so many people,' José opined, struggling to make sense of the ripples of excitement stirring through the tightly-packed horde. He caught sight of the wobbling tips of a few pointy hats. 'What are they doing?' he asked. 'Where are they going?'

Fighting against the crowd and straining to see around a corner, Jaime's voice cut through the confusion. 'I don't know, José,' he yelled, answering truthfully, 'but it seems that the people with the hats are heading into the building with the large doors.'

It was frustrating; no sooner had the mighty doors been swung open, admitting the worthy into dark cavernous spaces, than they were closed, leaving a vacuum of hungry suspicion.

'*¿Y ahora, qué?*[50] asked a disappointed José, as wood closed on wood with a ponderous thud.

'Now we go to a bar,' Jaime told him. 'Come on, they're probably going to be locked away in there for hours. We've plenty of time for a beer or two.'

Needing little persuasion, José and Raquel followed Jaime into one of the narrow alleyways and soon found themselves ensconced in a small bar, niche-like and sandwiched between grimy yellow walls.

José was enjoying every minute; aside from Jaime, whose suggestions always seemed to be such good ones, no one was telling him what to do. Standing by the counter, he wrapped his hand round the *caña*[51] that had appeared in front of him and lifted it to his face.

'*¡Venga, venga, venga!*' he exhorted. '*¡Salut!*'

Noticing the animation on José's face and the excitement in his eyes, Jaime and Raquel lifted their glasses and said, '*Salut, José. Salut.*'

José gulped his beer, large eyes staring over the rim of the glass. He couldn't understand why Jaime and Raquel weren't downing their drinks as quickly. Never mind, he thought, and, not wanting to miss anything, upended the glass, drained it, and smacked it onto the marble-topped bar. The noise rea-woke the interest of his elders, who once again focused their attention on Jaime's little brother.

'José?' they asked, both at the same time. 'What are you doing?'

'Pee,' he replied. 'I need to pee.' He jumped off the stool and went off in search of the lavatory.

'Are we having another, or what?' he asked as soon as he returned to the bar.

'We are, José,' came the reply. 'You're not. We got you a coke.'

'A coke? A *coke*? Where's my beer?' José was distraught at the idea of being left out of things, whatever they were. 'I want another beer, why can't I have another beer? I de*mand* another beer.'

'José, quieten down. You've had enough,' Jaime told him. 'We've still got the evening ahead of us, and the parade and everything. You need to stay on your feet.'

'Maybe you can have one later,' Raquel said, feeling pity for the youngster.

'Maybe,' Jaime agreed, shaking his head.

The irregular angles of Puerta Nueva were shrouded in a blanket of silence; dramatic after the noise of the street sweepers, scratching dustily through encroaching dusk, had faded into echoing alleys.

'Why are they sweeping the streets at this time of day?' José asked.

A woman, overhearing his question, supplied the answer. 'They have to make sure the way is clear for the *costaleros*,' she told him. 'It would be dangerous if one of them tripped and fell.'

'*¿Costaleros?*' he asked.

'The bearers,' she explained. 'The people who carry the Virgin.'

Suddenly, the streetlights went out and the tall buildings closed in, and from somewhere came the sound of the hand bell. A gothic squeak from a dry hinge amplified itself hugely as it bounced off opposing façades and gave a hint of something very large and very heavy being moved. The bell rang again, one medium sized ring between a "*ding*" and a "*dong*", a frequency just strong enough to motivate the procession; which all made sense because now José had found a stumpy concrete pillar to stand on and, fingers entangled in Jaime's hair, his balancing act enabled him to see over the dark blobby heads that that's what it was.

'A parade, a parade, Jaime, it's a big parade,' José enthusiastically informed his brother.

Everywhere, there were candles and all of them were moving, slowly, majestically, magically, until José's eyes sucked in enough light to realize they were being carried by tall pointy-headed shapes, and there were eyeholes, yes, two eyeholes in each upside down cone. José was a little uncertain about all this and tightened his grip on his brother's head.

'José!' Jaime squawked in pain.

'Ssshhh,' the crowd hissed in annoyance.

José stared at the huge float easing out between the massive doors; he stared and reckoned the whole contraption was on fire. Reflected candlelight seethed around the gaudy excess of Christianity, a million drops of molten flame embracing the vision. Laden with geegaws and trinkets, jewel-encrusted diadems, gold and silver-threaded tapestries and chains of pearls, the whole ensemble, oscillating minutely from side to side, mirrored the shower of imagined fiery globules as they cascaded earthwards.

Again, the sound of a bell as the entourage began its lumbering passage through the crowded square. Entranced, José didn't pause to wonder if the bell was used to clear the way of intended progress or if it was just a method of keeping time for the marching feet, it was all the same to him and, metronome or not, the enthroned young Virgin glided inexorably forward. Following five hundred years of zealous pageantry, the procession oozed painfully across the square and José found himself rubbing noses with a phalanx of hooded penitents. And then, in the midst of the devotional milieu, he saw her, the beautiful girl who earlier in the evening had touched his heart and fired his imagination into orbit.

Loosening his stranglehold on Jaime's hair and indifferent to his pious neighbours, all mumbling religion with the attitude of praying mantises, José leapt from his perch. 'Come on!' he yelled. 'We have to follow.'

'Why?' asked Raquel.

'Why?' asked Jaime.

'Because I saw her, she's there!' José exclaimed, unable to contain himself.

'Who?' asked Raquel.

'Who?' asked Jaime.

'The girl, the girl, the pretty girl,' José told them, amazed at their stupidity.

12. Evening

José belched loudly and in so doing, woke himself up.

'You're back again, then?' María observed.

'Never went away,' José responded.

'What *were* you dreaming about?'

'Dreaming?'

'You had an enormous erection, a tent pole standing up in your trousers,' María told him, eyes twinkling with merriment.

'Oh,' said José, unsure whether he should be embarrassed or proud.

'Well?' María persisted.

'Well, what?'

'Who was it, then? Who managed to work you up into such a state?' she asked.

'You, you silly woman,' José answered. 'It was you. You were dressed all in red, holding a candle.'

'Yes dear, of course I was,' María condescended, wondering where José's dreams had taken him.

'I'm starving,' José announced.

'*Comme toujours*,' María countered, using her fancy expression. 'I will never understand how a man who does so little, can eat so much.'

José folded his hands over his belly and moodily surveyed the tabletop. Fully awake, he noticed with some curiosity the pictures that seemed to be emanating from the shiny plastic surface. Raising his eyes, he discovered the images to be reflections of the luminous television screen, showering the sleeping patio with incessant information.

'You've cleared everything away,' he said, wiping an extended forefinger through the shamble of technicoloured randomness. 'It's all clean.'

'Yes, José, good of you to notice.'

Grabbing the edge of the table with his left hand and his stick with his right, José dragged himself to his feet. 'I'm going to stretch my legs,' he said, tugging at an earlobe. 'Five minutes.'

Stumbling stiffly across the patio, José hauled himself up the slight rise to the track running behind the cottage and came to a standstill. Undecided about whether to turn left, downhill, or to follow the dusty lane in the other direction, towards the east, he raised his head and sniffed the evening air; it was cooler now and laden with the sickly aroma of overripe figs. Arbitrarily, José turned towards the west and gazed into the distance, across the valley with its lake, dark and mysterious, and across the scattered hills stretching towards a line of mountains and the setting sun, a large squat orange seeking sanctuary below the ragged horizon. The view was truly staggering and despite having lived here all his life, José never tired of it. He stood motionless, as he had on countless other evenings – a man leaning heavily on his cane in the centre of a dusty track in the middle of nowhere – and marvelled at the world spread at his feet.

To his left, no further than a crow's flight of six or seven kilometres, he could make out the coastline, a long stretch of gently vibrant Mediterranean, neatly bisected by a hill crowned with the ruins of Bentomiz Castle. On his right, to the north, stood the sentinel, Maroma, the highest mountain in the chain that separated this tranquil oasis from the rest of the country.

José glanced at the sleeping giant, its outline indistinct in the rapidly gathering dusk, and shivered involuntarily at stark memories of a momentous escape into the mountains above Canillas. He used the tip of his stick to push at a large stone that sat defiantly in his way. Manoeuvering the hindrance haphazardly towards the edge of the track, he thought back to the titanic struggle that had torn his country apart. He recalled vividly the headlong flight when he and a couple of friends had been forced to flee Franco's ruthless régime, and now, ambling through early twilight, he tried to make sense of it all, past and present, the sheer desperation, hatred, fanaticism or whatever it was that moved people's hearts and made them do atrocious things, the specific mindset that last week had the power to send those terrorists on their one-way mission.

'Sheer stupidity,' he told the evening air, remembering the conversation that had ebbed and flowed over the lunch table. 'You don't do something like that without expecting consequences, it's nothing short of a declaration of war.' José thought back to the last time the world had found itself at crisis point – Kennedy, Krushchev, the '61 fiasco of the Bay of Pigs – the height of the Cold War, a time when atomic annihilation had seemed imminent. He spent a few moments working it out; forty years, and, stuck in a groove, recalled the idiot, the same generalissimo idiot who, after thirty odd years had still been in charge of Spain, José's own beloved Spain. In those days all the news had came out of the little radio that now lived on a shelf in the garage, gathering dust. In those days not many people had owned a television set. He recalled the occasion when he'd arrived at the cottage clutching the brand new apparatus made in England by someone called Maraconi, that's the way he always pronounced it, and remembered how fascinated he'd been when watching the scratchy black-and-white pictures of that astronaut stepping onto the moon; what was his name? José flicked another sizeable stone into the undergrowth – Armstrong, that was it.

Deep in space, he tilted his head backwards and stared at the velvet sky and the few bright diamonds that had dared to pitch their strength against the diminishing power of Sol. The moon was still in hiding and while José stared at the stars, his neck complaining at strange angles, he realized that ever since 1969 he'd been hooked on all things celestial, had even found a children's book that furnished him with more information than he really needed to know. He'd pushed his brain through slingshots and precession and gravity and had scratched at the weirdness of black holes, often wondering what it would be like to fall into one. But he loved the moon, silver, yellow, pink, and blood-orange when it popped up, fat on the eastern horizon. He would gaze at Earth's little sister in all her forms and marvel at the fact that there were footprints embedded for eternity in her grey dusty seas.

José stood on the edge of the firmament, unbuttoned his flies and aimed at dark shadows, humming vaguely while he waited for something to happen. He farted as he worked his muscles and remembered how María had told him it was because of all the beer he consumed, something about the gas having to escape. He'd retorted, saying it was nothing to do with the beer, that it was something natural, something that became more natural the older you got, and reminded her that he'd been farting for sixty years. And that's when María, having told him she didn't need reminding, had been quick to point out that he'd been drinking for sixty years.

He grinned at the moon and waited.

A startled rabbit scampered away across the rough ground and disappeared into the wilderness, a sizeable plot of land untended for many years, an area of scrub and long grasses. Something bright and shiny peered at him out of the gloom – a discarded empty cigarette packet, its cellophane wrapper catching the dying twinges of daylight. José flicked at it with his cane and sent it flying into the wasteland where it would lie undisturbed for years to come, losing its lustre and disintegrating slowly, a curiosity for wildlife.

'And that's another problem,' he muttered, directing a feeble flow towards some overgrown fennel. 'There'll be nobody around to look after all this land.'

He turned on his heel and headed homeward, thinking about the discussion he'd had with Manolo, yesterday, or had it been last week? Unable to remember with any certainty when the conversation had taken place, the more he thought about it, he realized it had been more of a monologue, a long rambling outpouring as Manolo had complained about his useless children and how none of them had any interest in the land.

'You know?' José said, sitting in his chair, watching María pour some home-grown wine into a glass. 'We've been lucky with

Vicente.'

'Now what are you talking about?' María asked.

'Vicente, we've been lucky,' José told her, rearranging the order of words. He waited while María ladled rabbit stew onto his plate, three large scoops of meat, onions, carrots and potatoes in thick gravy, mostly gravy, the choice lumps of meat and vegetables having been consumed in a previous lifetime. From another plate he took a slice of bread, folded it in half and squashed it into the insubstantial sauce.

'He likes the land,' José announced.

'Yes dear, of course he likes the land,' María agreed, serving herself with some of the leftover hotpot.

'I mean, he *likes* the land, you know? As opposed to not liking it,' José said, endeavouring to clarify the point.

Looking across the table, María viewed her husband in the way that all wives view their husbands when waiting to be told something that is outrageously obvious. Withering.

'Well, Manolo's kids don't,' José finished smugly.

'I know,' María said equably.

'You know?' José asked, astonished. 'How do you know?'

'*Hombre*, it's common knowledge. We women, when we're not busy cooking, cleaning, sewing or painting, we . . . Well, we get together and gossip. Deep discussions we have, José. Deep discussions.'

'How? When?'

'Ooh, often enough. Maybe once a week,' María told him, teasing, drawing out her responses.

'Goodness, woman! What *do* you talk about?' José demanded, exasperated.

'Just about everything. You'd be surprised at the some of the conversations we have.'

'But I've never seen you in deep discussion . . . except maybe on Wednesdays, you know, at the market?'

'Hmm, we like to talk about things other than babies, weddings, snoring husbands and hand-me-downs.'

'But . . .'

'You know?' María said, fixing José with a determined stare. 'There's one thing I've never spoken about with anyone. Never. Not a word.'

José stared straight back, waiting, tired eyes unblinking in the dim light cast by the patio lantern.

'Laia,' María stated.

'Laia?' José asked. 'Laia?'

'Laia,' María repeated. 'Your mother told me, the night before we were married.'

'My mother?' José asked. 'What did she tell you? And who's Laia?'

'Who's Laia?' María echoed, shaking her head. 'Who's Laia?' After a short pause and with faltering voice, she continued, 'Laia was the sister you never had.'

'Sister?' José asked, confused.

'It was a secret,' María answered, 'such a big secret. No one knows about it, no one. When your parents died, the secret died with them.'

'I had a sister?' José asked, astounded. He picked up his cane and used it to prod at the television. He managed to locate the off button and watched, tight-lipped, as the doomsday pictures from the other side of the world faded into a tiny bright spot, and died.

'I had a sister?' he repeated, more slowly.

'No, José, you didn't . . .'

'But you . . .'

'Oh, José, I shouldn't have told you.'

'Yes, María,' José said, taking her hands in his, 'you should, you have to.'

'I should've kept it to myself,' María continued, not listening. 'Like your mother and father kept it to *them*selves.'

'You have to, María,' José implored. 'You must tell me everything.'

'I wish I'd never started,' María lamented.

José raised an arm and used a big clumsy hand to wipe away a tear that had started to roll down one of María's plump cheeks. 'You have to tell me,' he told her quietly. 'It's out now, out in the open, and I want to know everything.' Moving his hand away from María's face, he placed the arm around her shoulders and drew her towards him, letting her head nestle into the crook of his neck. Enveloped in autumn twilight, they sat and listened to the cicadas calling to one another across the brooding brittle stillness. Even the dogs, which normally spent the evenings snuffling about the patio, had given up and gone to sleep, sleek heads resting on nervous paws.

'She didn't know if it was a girl,' María said, almost a whisper. 'It was your mother's imagination that somehow . . . oh I don't know, somehow made it not be a boy, I suppose.' She picked a piece of kitchen paper off the table and used it to dab at her eyes. 'Having convinced herself that she was going to have a baby girl, she gave it a name . . . Laia.'

María blew her nose into the damp piece of paper.

'It's so sad, José,' she said, turning to face him, 'so sad. And they never said anything to you? You didn't know?'

'No,' José replied. 'I didn't know.'

'Your mother, when she told me, was able to laugh about it. She said they had a huge fight and that your papa was well out if it.'

'He was?'

'Yes,' María answered, 'he'd been drinking heavily. It was *feria* week or something. I can't remember exactly what Inmaculada said, perhaps it was a festival or some special occasion. Anyway, he'd been out all night, your father, and when he came home they went at it hammer and tongs. Your mother reckoned she almost killed him.'

'What?' José asked.

'A real humdinger,' María explained. 'Plates flying, lots of swearing; they even drew blood.'

'*¡Joder!*' José remarked, breaking the word into two heavily stressed syllables. He looked at his plate, contemplated the forgotten stew and used a chunk of bread to manoeuvre a fragment of meat, a wedge of potato and a morsel of well-cooked carrot onto his fork. He shovelled the food into his mouth and chewed absentmindedly, his mouth opening and closing in the manner of grotesque machinery.

Still munching and still grasping the fork in his clenched fist, he glanced at María, and beyond at the flickering lantern. He watched a large moth dancing in a fragile penumbra, attracted by the light, repelled by the heat. He grunted and used his left hand to raise the glass of wine to his mouth, lips pouting anticipation towards the tilting rim. Suddenly, he stopped, lowered the glass and set it back on the table.

'I was there,' he said softly, in dawning realization. 'Bloody hell, I was there.'

13. Honeymoon

José opened the window, breathed deeply and sampled the air. He noticed it to be a little cooler, but this was to be expected in the Sierra del Valle, the range of mountains he could see stretching into the distance. Crossing the room to the other window, he gazed with awe at another colossus, an enormous slab of granite rising sheer from a forest of pine trees. Everywhere, mountains and pine trees, and in the distance, a glint of blue.

José had never travelled so far in his life, and the whole of the previous day had been spent toiling along hot dusty roads. A succession of various forms of transport had taken turns in delivering José and María to Málaga, and an ancient bus, wheezing and coughing at every bend along the way, had brought them to the lakes. It hadn't taken long before José had become impatient; in fact it had happened shortly after they'd left Málaga.

*   *   *

'Why are we stopping here?' José had asked María as they looked out of the bus at a ramshackle collection of houses strung along the side of the road. 'Anyway, where *are* we?'

They turned their attention to the view offered by the window on the other side of the bus, and saw nothing. The empty land stretched away towards distant hills, barren, save for an occasional palm or eucalyptus, brave champions standing proud in the withered earth.

José looked at the old man who'd just boarded the bus, regarded him with suspicion. '*¿Dónde estamos?*[52] he demanded.

'Campanillas,' the man replied, clutching a chicken under his left arm.

'Campanillas?' José asked. He'd never heard of the place.

'*Sí*,' came the response as the bus rattled into active mobility. The man settled himself and his chicken onto a seat on the other side of the aisle.

'Where's Campanillas?'

'Málaga,' the man replied, 'it's near Málaga.'

'It can't be,' José protested. 'We left Málaga ages ago.' He looked at María who was looking out of the window, watching the world creep by. 'Didn't we?'

María turned to face him, raised an eyebrow.

'He says we're still not far from Málaga,' José informed her, 'but we can't be.'

'Why?' María asked.

'Why?' José asked, before repeating himself. 'Why?'

He looked through the window at the dilapidated houses, one after the other steadily moving out of view as the driver crunched gears. Then they were gone, replaced by open landscape. Suddenly, he had another idea. 'Where are you going?' he asked the man across the aisle.

'Alora,' came the answer.

'How far's Alora?' José enquired. 'I mean, how long will it take to get there?'

'Hard to say,' the man replied. 'Depends.'

'Depends? Depends on what?'

'Depends on how often we have to stop,' the man answered, grinning widely.

José could have launched a tight knuckled fist across the aisle. He had no idea where Alora was and didn't really care, although he started to think that someone had told him the place was about halfway between Málaga and the lakes.

'Well, how long does it usually take?' he asked, returning the man's smile despite feeling far from cheerful. In fact, he felt pretty uneasy. His stomach was in turmoil and he began to wish he hadn't consumed so much alcohol the night before. Still, he consoled himself, it's not every day I get married.

'¿Qué?[53] He realized he'd missed the man's answer.

'No sé,' the man replied.

'What do you mean, "you don't know"? You must know.' José felt exasperation crawling up his gullet.

'This is my first trip,' the lopsided smile replied.

'¡Joder!' José exclaimed. He leaned his head against María's shoulder and tried to think of something nice, something to take his mind off the rebellion that seemed to be fomenting within. Something began poking at his arm and he looked down to see the chicken making an all-out assault. He grabbed the bird and shoved it back across the great divide. 'Here,' he said, full of angst and pissed-off indignation, 'try to control this thing.'

The man from Campanillas took hold of the proffered animal. 'I know someone,' he said, looking at José conspiratorially.

'You do,' José agreed.

'Yes,' the man nodded.

José shook his head. 'And?'

'This person I know . . .'

'Yes,' José coaxed, thinking of dentists and teeth.

'He travels a lot, knows all the buses.'

'But does he travel on *this* bus?' José asked on the verge of giving up.

'Yes.'

'And?' José enquired from the top of the wall he'd been forced to climb.

'About two hours.'

'What?' José yelled. The wall collapsed and every head in the bus turned to locate the source of commotion. José was beyond caring. 'Two hours? Two hours to get from here to Alora? That means . . .'

'Two hours,' the man with the chicken confirmed, nodding his head in measured gravitas.

'Two hours,' José groaned. 'Two whole hours, it'd be quicker on a horse and cart.' He watched the chicken as it pecked at some seeds the man was holding in the palm of his hand. 'Two hours,' he said to María. 'That means four hours until we get to the hotel. I think I'll be dead by then.'

María took hold of his hands. 'The bus stops for an hour when it gets to Alora,' she told him, 'the driver will have to take a break. We can have a rest, too.'

'But that's a*noth*er hour,' José complained. 'Too much resting, we'll never make it.'

María leaned against the window, pulled José's head onto her shoulder. 'We'll make it,' she replied, 'besides, we're on honeymoon. There's no hurry.'

They'd arrived eventually at half-past eight, the owner of the hotel fussing over them, effusive, and at the end of a long journey, annoying.

'I've given you room 317, it's beautiful, it's the best. There's a bathroom close by on the landing and the view is magnificent.'

'From the landing?' José asked, incredulously.

'No, from the bedroom,' came the reply, honest, straight and innocent. 'It's the best view in the area, absolutely the best, and if you open the windows,' the owner hastened on, 'the room will be kept cool by mountain breezes.'

'Mountain breezes,' José agreed, nodding his head, more in exhaustion than an attempt to keep the conversation flowing.

They followed the host up a staircase and along a couple of corridors, all the while listening to a discourse on the beauty of the surrounding area and the benefits to be gained from inhaling deeply the pure, healthy, pine-fresh air.

Once the door had been closed, José and María collapsed in a heap onto the large matrimonial bed and would have stayed there, immobile, had it not been for the gentle but insistent rapping that forced José to stagger back to the door and open it.

A maid, bearing an enormous tray, stood on the thresh-old. 'Compliments of the hotel,' she announced shyly, almost curtseying, dimpled rosy cheeks displaying profound embar-rassment or perhaps just a living advertisement for the healthy lifestyle to be found in the mountains. She offered the tray forward towards José, who had no choice but to accept the hotel's gift of food and drink.

'*Gracias*,' he said to the figure that was retreating backwards through the doorway. '*Muchísimas gracias*.'

*   *   *

José returned to the north-facing window and stood staring into the distance. 'I'm starving,' he announced, turning to watch his wife of forty-two hours climb out of bed.

To his left, resting on a chair, last night's tray paid testimony to the fact that the travellers had been too tired to pay much attention to food – a dried-up, half-eaten sandwich lay on a bed of wilting lettuce leaves, the platter decorated with a confetti of tired crisps.

A knock at the door brought him full circle and he strode across the room to open it.

'*Desayuno*,' said the maid, the same fresh-faced girl of the night before. She placed the breakfast tray on a table, scooped up the other tray bearing the un-eaten supper, and retreated, leaving José to close the door behind her.

'*Magia*,'[54] he said, lifting a chunk of bread and two slices of salami towards his mouth.

'Not so much magic,' María told him, 'as . . .'

'Necessity,' José finished, crashing the end of María's sentence.

'What shall we do?' María pondered, setting her coffee cup onto the tray. She looked up and smiled. 'I mean, here we are in the middle of nowhere and . . .'

'The gorge, the gorge,' José answered, boyish excitement clouding newfound maturity. 'We're going to see the gorge.'

'The gorge?' María asked. 'What gorge?'

'You know, the gorge, the King's Walk and everything?

202

Dad's always going on about it. You must've heard him?'

'I don't think so,' María responded.

'You must have,' José insisted, 'it's his abiding interest. Has been since it was built about twenty years ago. Anyway,' he added, a little uncertainly, 'it's one of the world's wonders.'

'Is it?' María asked, eyes wide open.

'Well,' José replied, moderately scaling down the importance of his statement and that of the airy walkway, 'it's one of Andalucía's. Anyway,' he continued, 'it's s'posed to be amazing, and all these dams and things . . . well, Papa says it's all to do with electricity.'

'Elec*tri*city!' María exclaimed. 'Sounds really interesting.'

'No, no, there's nature and lakes as well,' José enthused, throwing some clothes at his wife. '*And* the King's Walk. Come on.'

'Can't wait,' María replied through a mouthful of bread and cheese, whilst hoisting a skirt up her legs. 'Electricity!'

El dueño[55] was ecstatic. '*Si, si, señor, estupendo; y tenéis suerte.*'[56] He slammed his hand onto the brass bell that virtually dominated the reception desk. 'Marta,' he said to the maid who arrived as the sound of the bell evaporated into space. 'Marta, run quickly and catch the milk lorry.'

Fixing José and María with a huge grin, he said, '*Señor y señora*, you will have a fantastic day. The lorry will take you to the other end of the gorge. From there you will walk back via the Caminito del Rey. You will continue alongside a lake and through a forest and then you will go through a tunnel. Here,' he continued, handing a well-creased piece of paper across the counter, 'is a map.'

Marta, face redder than ever, returned from her errand

only to be sent to the kitchen to prepare a picnic. 'Hurry, hurry,' she was directed.

José and María went outside and stood in bright sunlight, watching as the milk lorry reversed through a great cloud of oily smoke. The driver pulled at an obstinate brake handle, removed a pack of cigarettes from behind the visor and, happy to have a couple of minutes in which to do nothing, leapt out of the cab.

'*Hola*,' he said, walking up to the steps that led down from the hotel's entrance. '*¿Cómo estáis?*[57]

'*Bueno. Muy bueno*,' José replied; and that was that.

The driver walked away and sat himself on a low wall that stopped the road from plunging into a ravine. Crosssing his legs, he lit a cigarette and studied the ground in front of him.

Forty-five minutes later, José and María stood side by side and watched the lorry, trundling ahead of its plume of smoke, disappear . . . and reappear, as it followed the twists and turns in and out of the mountain folds along the road to Alora.

José was in his element, surrounded by countryside, surrounded by nature. Taking hold of María's hand, he led her to the edge of the river and together they strode purposefully across the mighty dam.

Following the directions of *el dueño*, they climbed to the tiny station at El Chorro and started walking along the line towards the towering mountains. After a short distance, a sturdy iron bridge brought them face to face with a gaping hole bored into the side of the mountain. It was here that they left the track and joined the southern end of the nerve-wracking King's Walk. María baulked at the sight of the path, a narrow concrete ledge stapled to the face of perpendicular cliffs that for millions of years have shrouded the awe-inspiring depths of the Desfiladero de los Gaitanes.

'José,' she said, pressing herself firmly against solid rock. 'José, I can't.'

José had gone on ahead and was nearing a fearsome wooden bridge that stretched precariously across the chasm. 'Yes, María, yes you can,' he urged. 'It's easy, just don't look down and you'll be okay. Come on, I'll wait for you.' Disregarding his own advice, José peered into the abyss and saw the dark swirling waters surging through the defile a hundred metres below. He swallowed in nervous comprehension of the grandiose immensity of raw nature. 'Take it slowly, hold onto the rail and you'll be fine,' he said, directing the encouragement at himself as well as at his wife.

A few minutes later, heart in mouth, María stood once again beside her husband. 'I don't think I'm enjoying this,' she said quietly, looking at the bridge and its collection of vague filaments. 'I don't think I like it, being so high. It's too dangerous.'

'It's okay,' José said, taking a few precious tentative paces. 'Look, I'm nearly halfway across, already.'

María glanced at José, then returned to her study of the bridge, contemplating the construction, wondering at its strength, its safety.

'You go on,' she instructed. 'When you're safely across, I'll follow.'

She looked upwards to where the towering cliffs almost met, eighty metres above her head. She looked up beyond the rocks, beyond the buzzards floating lazily on the thermals; she looked into the deep blue skies and silently made the sign of the cross.

Her gaze swept back to the bridge in front of her, to her husband waiting for her on the other side. How apt, she thought to herself, if this bridge collapses or if I fall off, it'll be me who's waiting on the other side. She raised her head, took a deep breath and walked serenely across the fragile structure.

It was fantastic. Unnerving, but fantastic. María recovered from her apprehension and José didn't admit to having had any in the first place. Following the narrow path, they wound in breathless suspension above the sinuous canyon. On one or two occasions, coming upon places where the railway broke from deep seclusion within the opposing cliff, they felt they could reach out and touch the tracks, gleaming rods of steel fusing into the monstrous façade, pinning it together in man's feeble attempt to reunite nature with the material he'd torn out of it.

After a kilometre of winding intimidation, they thought they'd never reach the end, but the gorge steadily began to widen and opened eventually into a deep valley blocked by another dam. Exhausted after their hike and the adrenalin rush that kept them glued to the safety of the path, they decided to stop for a while and sat on the edge of the gently curving concrete construction.

Sitting in the heat of the midday sun, their legs swinging a few centimetres above placid waters, José and María relaxed and looked about them; at the wall of reeds fringing the lake on either side and at the pine trees ranged along the edges of the valley until, reaching rocky heights, their roots could find no anchor. To the accompanying sound of chattering water, they sat in peaceful enchantment, holding hands and exchanging passionate kisses.

'Hey! What are you doing on my dam?'

The voice rang out loud and clear from somewhere to the right.

'Your dam?' José asked somewhat suspiciously, trying to locate the man's location.

'My land,' the man answered, stepping out from behind a large boulder. He was tall and dark-skinned and despite seeming quite elderly, appeared to be in good shape. 'All this is my land,' he added, arms held out as if encompassing the whole valley. Advancing towards them down the rock-strewn hillside, he turned and pointed back along the way he'd come, 'And those are my sheep.'

José looked in the direction indicated and saw a small flock of sheep and a few goats ruminating on a patch of rocky ground. As he watched, the man took a leather sling from under his belt, balanced a pebble in the centre and hurled it towards the animals. The sound of the stone striking a tree caused a couple of stray sheep to emerge from cover and join the rest of the flock.

'Pretty good,' José remarked, getting to his feet as the shepherd approached. 'I suppose you get a lot of practice?'

'All day, every day,' the man answered gruffly. 'So, what are you doing?'

'We just got married,' María told him.

José looked at her and shuffled his feet.

'Married? Here? On my dam?' the shepherd enquired, astonishment in his eyes.

'No,' José replied. 'A long way from here, in the mountains the other side of Málaga.'

'Málaga! That *is* a long way,' the shepherd agreed. He removed his flat cap, scratched the top of his head and then replaced the tatty piece of fabric. 'You walk here?'

'Yes,' María answered.

'No,' José said at the same time. 'Well, yes, *and* no. We walked here from the gorge but a bus brought us to the hotel,' he explained.

The shepherd stared at both of them as if undecided about whether he should allow these strangers to stay on his territory.

Suddenly, María remembered the picnic they'd brought with them. 'Come and sit with us and share some food,' she said, stepping off the dam and heading towards a patch of sheep-cropped grass. She sat on the ground and began unwrapping the small parcel of supplies, a simple fare of bread, cheese, salami, a couple of apples and some apricots. At the bottom of the bag she discovered two bottles of beer.

'Looks like you got yourselves a feast,' their newfound friend informed them, settling himself slowly onto the ground. 'Going down's not too bad,' he grimaced, 'it's the getting up again that's the trouble.'

José pulled the bung from one of the bottles and passed the beer to the shepherd.

'A rare treat,' the old man confessed, smiling. Raising the bottle to his mouth, he looked around at the land he loved and had known for most of his life, his eyes mere slits against the glare of the sun. He looked up at the craggy peaks, sharp against the deep blue sky, and watched the buzzards to see if they were gathering, a sure sign that one of his animals would be in danger. Then, mind at ease, he returned the bottle to José and attached his attention to the couple whose food he was eating. 'You country folk?' he asked.

'Yes,' José replied, 'but different country. Grapes and

olives, and almonds too.'

'Flat?'

'No,' José said, nodding and shaking his head at the same time. 'Like this, hills and mountains.' He looked at the peaks soaring above his head. 'Maybe not so high.'

'Not so high,' the shepherd agreed, sagely.

Just then, a rumbling sound came from somewhere behind them. Alarmed, José and María rose to their feet and looked in all directions, trying to ascertain what kind of animal would be responsible for making this strange noise. Seeing nothing, they looked to the shepherd for a sign, some sort of assurance that all was well. Evidently without a care in the world, he was still sitting, legs stretched out in front of him, bottle of beer halfway to his mouth. He looked at the two strangers, saw their anxiety and started laughing, loud guffaws ringing around the hills and blending with the heavy rumbling which, second by second, was intensifying.

When they thought it could get no louder, a mighty hissing as from a thousand dragons, spewed out of the mountain from somewhere a short distance above them. María and José were quick to clap their hands over their ears, but the roaring and the rumbling rattled their bones and left them wide-eyed and gasping, wondering why they'd chosen to come and sit here, on what surely must be the edge of some long forgotten volcano.

Then, the beast was gone, its breath fading away, and the valley returned to peaceful existence. The sounds of nature crept into audibilty; the call of a bird, the bleating of a sheep or goat, and the constant murmur of cascading water as it rippled through a channel in the centre of the dam . . . and from the shepherd, peals of cackling laughter.

José and María had been cowering in terror and only now did they begin to recover, trying desperately to compose themselves by coming to terms with the fact that they'd survived some terrible ordeal.

'It was a train,' the shepherd gasped between shrieks of laughter.

'A train?' José asked, disbelief evident in his voice.

'A train,' the shepherd repeated. 'There's a small access into the tunnel.' He turned and pointed. 'Just up there, behind those bushes.'

José and María craned their heads towards the group of shrubs, maybe a hundred metres away.

'We have to see this,' José declared, clutching one of María's hands, dragging her up the hill to find the tunnel.

A few minutes later and out of breath, they arrived at a stone archway leading into darkness.

'*Hombre*,' María whispered, hiding behind José as they stood on the periphery, 'it's so black.'

'You have to let your eyes get adjusted,' the shepherd told them as he came up to the entrance.

The three of them stood gazing into nothingness, watching the blackness grow fuzzy at the edges before it turned into a dusky grey. They could just make out the track, a dull gleam in the underworld, and in front of them, almost under their feet, a shimmer of water trickling through a culvert parallel to the line.

'It's scary,' said María. 'I wouldn't want to go in there.'

'It's my roadway,' said the shepherd, stepping into the tunnel, 'far quicker than walking over the mountains. I'll be home before you get anywhere near your hotel.'

'How can you see where you're going?' José asked. 'And

what happens if a train comes along?'

'Like I said, your eyes get used to the darkness. And if a train comes along? Well, there's plenty of room in the ditch.'

He moved out of sight and José and María were left listening to the sound of receding footsteps crunching on sharp shingle.

María shivered. 'I couldn't do that,' she said. 'It's too dark.'

'You could if you had to,' José told her.

'Maybe, but I don't,' she responded truthfully and thankfully.

The walk along the edge of the lake was delightful. Leading through variegated woodland, the path followed the contour of calm waters and María and José found the going easy.

The woods were full of movement, birds and butterflies swooping lazily from branch to branch, flower to flower, and the air vibrant with the drone of pollen-carrying bees. There were squirrels here too, and María found them enchanting. She watched them cavort up and down the pines and became ecstatic when one of the small furry rodents boldly advanced to within a couple of metres from where she was standing.

'Look, José, it's standing on its little back legs, and look, look . . . it's holding its little hands together and staring at me.'

Never before had they seen such friendly little animals; certainly none had been encountered in the countryside where the olive and the almond held sway.

From time to time, pausing to look through tall swaying reeds at the sparkling expanse of water, they'd see the aftermath of a fish breaking surface, concentric rings spreading silently from the point of contact.

The trees gave shelter from the burning afternoon sun and here, where the path became a little wider, José slipped an arm about María's waist and drew her close to his side as they sauntered along. A few minutes later, they stopped, and peeping through the branches, looked up to the dizzying heights where dark-green crowns brushed against an azure sky. José grinned and swung María round to face him. Placing his arms around her back, he pulled himself against her body.

María lifted her face and looked into the deep, dark-brown eyes. Standing on tiptoe she kissed his forehead, his eyes, his nose and his mouth, tenderly at first and then passionately, succumbing to the intense feelings that churned within.

José lowered his wife to the ground and stood awkwardly while she began to remove her clothing. Unfastening her blouse, María sat up straight to take it off, then, twisting to one side, asked José to help unclip her brassiere. He lifted his hands and fumbled, large fingers unaccustomed to such delicate operations. Eventually, after much concentration, he succeeded in his task and María, holding the loosened cups in place over her breasts, turned her body towards him. Leaning backwards until prone on the ground, she raised her hips and suggested that José should undo the button at the side of her skirt and pull the garment to her feet. José showed no hesitation and a few seconds later, his wife, save for the bra clamped between hands and breasts and a flimsy piece of material shielding her loins, was lying naked in front of him.

Watching intently the movement of her husband's eyes as they roved up and down the length of her prostrate body, Maria giggled. 'Now you, my love,' she told him. 'Now it's your turn.'

José sat beside her and removed his boots, great big heavy things tied with metres of lace that seemed to take forever to undo. Slowly, one after the other, his two feet emerged into the light of day. He parked the boots neatly at one side of the path and stood up to take off his trousers. With smooth dexterity, he managed to extricate one leg but, in his haste, the other foot became entangled and almost threw him off balance. His shirt was no problem – he pulled it over his head without bothering to undo the buttons.

While José struggled to break out of his clothes, María divested herself of her undergarments, simply, efficiently, and watched as her husband danced about trying to remove his socks. Conscious of the fact that he was standing in the woods dressed only in a pair of pants, José sat down again, quickly, and turned to embrace his wife.

Stretched out unadorned in dappled sunlight, they made love in the cradle of Mother Nature. While deep dark waters shimmered beneath a cloudless sky, the sounds of the enveloping forest and the shivering of reeds and bulrushes became one with the murmurs and moans of the entwined couple.

In the late afternoon they lay side-by-side, head to foot, María resting her head uncomfortably, but happily, on José's feet. And while the heady essence of sex and sweat coiled and coalesced with the foetid breath of the undergrowth, they quietly savoured the pleasure they'd found in each other's bodies.

Later, they came to another tunnel, much smaller and much shorter than the one used by the shepherd. With no sign of rails, they imagined there'd be no possibility of a train hurtling out of darkness, and peering into the depths were just able to make out a small circle of light, perhaps fifty or sixty metres distant.

'No,' María said. 'I can't, I just can't.'

'You can,' José said, trying once again to show encouragement. 'Besides,' he added, 'it's a short cut.' He unfolded the map that had been given to them at the start of the day. 'Look,' he said, pointing at the crudely sketched plan, 'here's the path, here's the tunnel, and . . . here's the hotel.'

'I don't care,' María laughed. 'I'm not . . .'

She stopped mid-sentence as José, map fluttering in hands, strode fearlessly into the tunnel.

'Come on,' he said. 'It's easy.'

'*Joder*,' María muttered, ducking low as she launched herself into subterranean gloom. 'What about spiders and things?' she asked tremulously. 'What about snakes?'

'Any snakes will have fled at the approach of your footsteps,' José tossed casually over his shoulder. 'And at the sound of your voice.'

'What about spiders, then?'

'They'll be too busy holding onto their webs,' José answered hopefully. He too was a little uncertain about the shifty creatures with four pairs of legs.

'See? We made it!' he called triumphantly as they emerged a few moments later into hot, brilliant sunlight.

'We did,' María agreed, instantly forgetting her fear of snakes and spiders and the short dark passage through the hill. 'So where's the hotel?'

'Um . . . just around the corner,' José assured her. 'Plenty of time for a wash before dinner.'

At this time of year, late September, evenings in the mountains could become quite chilly, and with only one other couple staying at the hotel, dinner was being served in the smaller of two restaurants, warm and welcoming with a log fire burning in an enormous hearth.

José and María sat at a circular table not too far from the fireplace. The table had been laid with napkins and silver cutlery, and the tablecloth, hanging to the floor except where it draped over the diner's legs, cunningly trapped the heat from some coals nestled in a small metal dish beneath the table. A short stubby candle burned in the globe of a large brandy glass positioned at the centre of the table, the flame's motionless image echoing deep within two more glasses, both holding generous measures of a dark crimson wine, *Tempranillo*, robust and peppery from a region to the north of the peninsula.

Sharing similar tastes, they began the meal with shellfish soup, served with a basket of warm home-baked bread. For the main course they'd been persuaded, without too much difficulty, to try the house speciality – honey-basted roast-leg-of-lamb. A dish for two and cloistered between rosemary-covered roast potatoes and onions, it arrived on an enormous platter along with a side dish of broccoli and cauliflower.

After their hike through the mountains and the encounters, exhilarations and intoxications of the day, the newly-weds were ravenous and maintained a comfortable silence as they tucked into their meal. Discreet but attentive, the waiter refilled their glasses when necessary and remembered to ask if they'd like a carafe of water. There was no hurry and they took their leisure, and thirty minutes later, a well-cleaned leg-of-lamb gave singular testimony to the chef's expertise.

Later, as they drank their coffee, the waiter approached

the table and asked if they'd like *flans*[58] for dessert.

'*¿Por qué no?*'[59] María answered, smiling. 'The meal has been superb, so we might as well finish with a delicious dessert.'

José sluiced some wine back and forth between his teeth before allowing the liquid to fall down his throat. 'Did you notice the man's eyes?' he asked María.

'Who's?' she enquired, perplexed.

'Who's? Who's?' José exclaimed. 'Why, the shepherd's of course. They were so deep, so full of mystery, unfathomable like oceans; the oldest, wisest eyes in the world. I've never seen anything like them.'

'They were blue,' María conceded.

José reached out with his right hand and clasped tightly María's left, pressing it against the tablecloth and the fork with which she'd been toying. 'I know, I know,' he said, 'he was a shepherd, a man of the mountains, living with his sheep and his goats, living a life of simplicity, a life of freedom, but . . . '

'A man of wisdom, a sage and a prophet,' María suggested, quickly exhausting her reservoir of philosophical words.

'Exactly!' José exclaimed in agreement. 'It was as though he knew the answer to everything. He was so at peace with himself, so assured, so at one with life.'

'Well, he probably has a lot of time to ponder things,' María reasoned, 'and, apart from a few bleating animals, no distractions; nothing to get in the way of deep communion with the inner-self.' She smiled as she trawled through the world of mystic enlightenment.

'Just imagine,' José said, a little lost, a little wistful. 'Just imagine.'

'Yes,' María answered. '*He* wouldn't worry about how long

it takes a bus to reach its destination, he'd turn his mind to other things, other more important things.'

The desserts arrived, and José released María's hand so she could pick up the fork and slide it into the soft underbelly of the *flan*. Sweet, yet slightly bitter when they tasted the layer of dark caramel, it was like manna from heaven and rapidly disappeared.

'You know?' José mused, 'I should've liked to have spent more time with that shepherd, I'm certain he could've . . .'

The candle, static in its glass prison at the centre of the table, flickered suddenly as though dancing to an invisible force. It went out, and then relit itself. Glancing at the other couple in the almost deserted dining room, José noticed that their candle also had been extinguished, but had failed to relight.

The sound of a heavy door being opened caused the diners to look up, and a sudden inrush of cold air blew at a pair of heavy velvet drapes, which until that moment had been accomplishing splendid concealment, and forced them aside. The solitary candle soon gave up the unequal struggle, leaving the fireplace to become the sole source of illumination.

The door slammed shut, and as their eyes grew accustomed to diminished light, José and María became aware of a tall dark stranger standing next to their table. They were trapped; even if trepidation hadn't rooted them to the spot, there was nothing they could do.

Reaching deep into a coat pocket, the stranger pulled out an object and set it on the table. The object was small and dark and seemed to be alive, pinpricks of light vaguely discernible on or perhaps within its surface; fantastical, it was difficult to be certain. In the manner of a magician, the man pulled his sleeves up to the elbows and drew both hands, one to the right, one to the left, slowly through the air above the candle. Within seconds, the flame once again flickered into life and in capricious luminosity, José was able to see that the object was a stone, oval-shaped and smooth and appearing to burn from within. He looked up at the stranger and recognized the swarthy, deeply lined face.

'To the newlyweds,' the shepherd intoned, throwing more powder into the flame. 'May you be guided by love and blessed with peace.'

Crackling harshly within the confines of the brandy snifter, the powder sent a wreath of pale blue smoke crawling up and over the rim of the bulbous glass. The couple at the neighbouring table clapped their hands and raised their glasses towards José and María. 'Love and peace,' they chorused, while the waiter busied himself dragging a chair across the floor and setting it at José and María's table.

'We were just . . .'

'I know,' the shepherd said.

'We were talk . . .'

'I know,' the shepherd repeated.

'But, how?' José managed to ask.

'I know many things,' the shepherd replied. 'I know the ways of the world, I know magic.'

'But this . . .' José paused, indicating the pall of coloured smoke hovering above the table.

'Is amazing, is it not?' the shepherd asked, smiling benignly at his captivated audience.

'Yes,' José agreed. 'Amazing.'

'Not so,' the shepherd responded firmly, as a bowl of

soup was placed in front of him. 'Not so.'

José and María waited while their companion shook open a napkin, stuffed one corner into his collar and fanned the remainder over his shirt and jacket.

'Nothing is what it seems,' he said enigmatically, before proceeding to lift a spoonful of soup towards his mouth.

José, pensive, watched suspiciously as the spoon was tipped towards a notch hidden in the folds of the weather-beaten face. He studied the face, the dark craggy skin, the deep-set blue eyes and suddenly, he knew. 'You're the priest!' he exclaimed. 'You've got his eyes.'

The shepherd, spoon motionless midway between bowl and mouth, looked sideways at José. 'I'm the brother of the priest, José, and my eyes are my own.'

'He doesn't look anything like the priest,' María interjected.

'He does, he does, of course he does,' José insisted. 'It's the eyes.'

'But . . .' María began.

'No no, not him, not the one who married us, but the other one,' María, 'the other one; his brother,' José explained in a complicated yet enthusiastic rush, forgetting about the proximity of the soup-slurping dark stranger. 'He even talks like him, has the same voice. They say the same sort of things, words, phrases.'

'I'm confused,' María confessed.

'He jumped out at me, all dark and lost in the shadows of his hat,' José continued. 'Frightened me to death and then asked tricky questions.'

'Who, José? Who jumped out?'

'The priest, María, the priest.'

The shepherd had begun to shake, his body trembling as he tried to control his mirth. 'Yes,' he said, patting one of José's hands, 'yes, he told me all about that episode and the "arrangement" with your brother . . . Jaime? A good story José, a *great* story, and from a time when religion held more sway, a time when priests and dark robes were given a little more respect.'

María's large eyes swivelled backwards and forwards, wonder and amazement written in her expression. 'And the stone?' she asked.

'Ah yes, the stone.' The shepherd took another spoonful of soup, set down the spoon and wiped his mouth. 'Beer,' he said to the hovering waiter, who was trying to listen to the conversation and trying not to be obvious. The shepherd regarded José with a deeply penetrating stare, which José felt boring through the layers of bone protecting his brain.

'The stone, I'm afraid, must remain a secret,' the shepherd stated bluntly.

'But . . .'

'It'll bring you luck. Both of you.'

'But where did it come from?' María asked, looking into the depths of the radiating stone.

'I can tell you that it doesn't come from these parts,' the shepherd informed them, 'it's from a country far from here. However, I found it in the tunnel, years ago when I came here on sabbatical; about the time of the dams, I think.'

'So if it's not from here, where . . ?'

'Like I said, it must remain a secret.'

And again, José felt the intransigent potency of the man's stare, intense and intimidating.

'So. Now I will leave you,' the shepherd said, rising from

his chair. Moving away from the table, he sprinkled some more of the magic dust into the candle flame, and by the time the crackles and sparkles had died away, the shepherd had gone.

*   *   *

'Something's not right,' José announced, dipping a second *churro* into a mug of sweet hot chocolate.

María looked across the table, awaiting enlightenment.

'He knows too much,' José stated. 'How can anyone know so much?' The problem had kept him awake most of the night, frenetic brain activity with no result. He'd woken late to find María sitting on the edge of the bed, dressed and ready to go downstairs.

Sleepy and lost in thought, he took a bite at the soggy end of the fritter and chewed laboriously, granules of sugar decorating his lips. 'He must be one and the same,' he told María, 'has to be.'

'Yes dear,' María agreed calmly, annoyingly so, having benefited from eight hours of tranquil slumber.

'"Yes dear",' José mimicked, scratching an unshaven chin as the chambermaid waitress approached their table. Executing a sort of embarrassed miniature curtsey, she placed a small white envelope onto the plate at José's side. He picked it up, turned it over and used a stubby forefinger to tear open the sealed flap. He peered into the ragged opening and extracted a folded piece of paper.

'This'll be the bill, then,' he joked, smiling at María.

Unfolding the slip of paper, José frowned at a photograph that slid into his hands. 'It's the shepherd,' he said, regaining interest in life, 'and the priest. Both of them, together.' He passed the picture to María, who made a careful study of the image.

She looked up. 'So they *are* brothers,' she said.

'I don't understand,' José grumbled. 'Last night he seemed to say so much, but . . . but really, in the end, told us nothing.'

'But he did say they were brothers,' María pointed out, handing back the photograph, 'and here's the proof. After all, there's no reason for him to have been lying.'

'None that we know of,' José grudgingly admitted.

'So then,' María concluded, happy that the subject had been resolved. And then, remembering the piece of paper in which the photograph had been enclosed, she asked, 'What about the piece of paper?'

José picked it up and held it out to his wife. 'I'm too confused,' he said, 'too nervous. *You* look.'

María unfolded the paper, noticing that it appeared to have been torn from a book. The page featured a photograph of a rock, and underneath, a lot of small print. She started to read but gave up when she discovered it was a foreign language. Passing the page back to José, she smiled at him, dark eyes full of love. 'I think it's a picture of our stone, but I don't think it's going to reveal any secrets.'

José snatched the paper out of her hands and devoured the contents with his eyes.

'Look,' he said excitedly, 'there's some writing, some words, a name or something.' He jabbed at the collection of sentences below the picture and slowly, letter by letter, read out the first word, 'O p a l u s . . . hmm, Opalus, I wonder what that is? Sounds like some strange animal, or maybe . . . Maybe it's the name of the stone?' José's eyes followed the pointing

222

digit as it worked further along the line. 'Can't make out the rest though, it's all in some strange language.'

'Let me have another look,' María said, reaching for the piece of paper, suddenly realizing and vaguely hoping the strange language might be French. She inspected the unfamiliar words and could find nothing that resembled *comme toujours*.

'It's no good,' she confessed, 'there's nothing here that I can recognize.'

'Never mind,' said José, smiling at his wife, 'we'll just call it Opalus. Maybe, as the man said, it'll bring us luck.'

14. Dreams

José woke up in time to go to bed.

He felt exhausted and deflated and when he tried to raise his arms, his muscles seemed to have the strength of a stale marshmallow, which was strange since he'd spent most of the day enjoying an extended siesta. However, he didn't spend too much time thinking about this because there was something in his mouth, something large and furry, and then it started to move and he realized it was his tongue. He opened his eyes and sat up and the sudden change of position caused a gas bubble to release itself from the prison of his stomach. Eerie noises accompanied its passage through the oesophagus and on up through the windpipe, and by the time it reached José's mouth, the bubble had become large enough to flatten his puffy tongue and explosive enough to force its way out between a pair of flabby lips.

'Damn!' he exclaimed, as the putrid cloud expanded into the stillness of the night to do battle with the scent of *Dama del Noche*,[60] the fragrant climber that housed a colony of lizards. A startled dog raised one eye and decided to bark, which meant a further couple of dogs had to raise their eyes and bark in sympathy.

José fumbled and found a half-empty can of beer on the patio table. He picked it up and hurled it at the noisy guardians. '*¡Cállete!*' he yelled as the can crashed into the rim of the low surrounding wall, ricocheted into the heavy night air and performed a series of stunning cartwheels on a slow motion return to earth. The unstable contents accepted gravity's invitation to seek freedom and José watched, spellbound, while the gentle '*glug*' of escaping liquid had the effect of making him want to pee.

Maintaining normal nocturnal protocol, he dragged himself out of the chair, hobbled to the wall and unzipped his flies. For several long seconds, nothing was achieved, and José sighed deeply as night vision clicked in and tried unsuccessfully to penetrate the immediate horizon. Being the same age as his bladder, his eyes worked slowly and he had to wait while the focusing department went through the necessary gear changes. Finally, valves opened and a stream of warmth cut through the sound of rasping cicadas and gave José the longed-for-experience of blessed relief. And while golden threads pattered onto the parched earth, he raised his head in veneration to the ruler of the universe, his sight travelling through space and connecting with the creamy swathe of the Milky Way.

The flow weak, José's bladder took time to empty itself, so, arms crossed, he stood in idle contemplation of the fuzzy stars wheeling above his head. He pondered on the works of God because, for the life of him, he couldn't imagine who else or what else could have come up with such an involved scheme. And then he thought he saw an alien and the shock caused him to stop peeing. The ancient valve snapped shut and that was that, except it wasn't. When he realized the pin-prick of light moving through the heavens was a satellite, the valve relaxed in sneaky fashion and left him dribbling onto the parapet. The whole experience proved to be too much and while packing himself into his trousers, José reckoned that communion with the power of God and time and space called for a beer, and on top of that, the itsy bitsy notion of fear at things unknown had dried his throat more effectively than one of María's home-made pasties.

Turning away from the wall, his left foot came into contact with the beer can and sent it skittering noisily across the tiles, spitting the few remaining drops of alcohol as it skewed hither and thither until it found a resting place alongside a slumped dog.

Dreaming of enormous rabbits whose imaginary teeth were about to rip into its flank, the wretched canine woke up and immediately became a cartoon creature, a ball of spiky hair and high-speed legs. Then the barking began and the comrades-in-collars dutifully took up the call, but ceased as soon as the guilty leader of the pack received a swift smack from José's stick.

'¡*Fuera!*[61] he yelled at the jittery animals. '¡*Fuera!*'

José stumped into the safety of the unlit kitchen and opened the door of the tall old-fashioned American-style fridge. Outlined by a wedge of light released from the sighing compartment, he looked up and down the ranks of wire shelving and there, on a plate at the top, a salami and a half-eaten piece of *morcilla*[62] lay huddled in close proximity like two freshly-laid dog turds; and on the shelf below, a bowl containing something brown and sloppy stood in splendid ceramic isolation. José jammed a finger into the cold coagulum and tasted . . . hmm, María's rabbit stew, what was left of it. Next to the stew, a block of golden butter half sat on the rump of a black bull glazed into perpetual inactivity on the surface of a small yellow dish, and on the shelf below, a couple of fish, using one startled eye apiece, stared accusingly at the late night interloper, their tiny pointy teeth grinning stupidly at the huge lemon that shared their plate. And there, *por fin,*[63] on the bottom shelf, a clutch of cans of cheap Belgian lager, standing proud like little soldiers with nowhere to go, an army trapped in plastic webbing.

José bent forward and snatched up one of the troops, levering it upwards and sideways so that its neck snapped out of the noose. Straightening up, can in hand, he noticed two small dishes containing his favourites – roasted almonds and marinated olives. He transferred the beer and both dishes onto the small kitchen table and used the side of his foot to close the fridge door.

Wearily, José slumped onto the only chair available, and on peeling back the can's aluminium tab, realization dawned that since this was María's domain, hers and hers alone, more chairs would be an unnecessary clutter. He raised the can to his lips and poured cold beer into his mouth, relishing the buzz from miniscule bubbles as they burst against his tongue. He picked a nut from one of the dishes, a couple of olives from the other and, chewing meditatively, noticed a bottle of Ponche Cabellero standing in silvered attention on top of the fridge.

'Hah!' he exclaimed, jumping up with alacrity belying age and fatigue.

In one grand balletic moment, José scooped a glass from the hotchpotch collection on the draining board to the left of the sink, collected the precious bottle from its perch on the fridge and returned to his place of sweet contemplation. But no, damn it, there was something missing – ice, he needed ice. Galvanized into action and with the taste of mellow Ponche reaching for his tongue, he returned to the outsize fridge, opened the door and yanked open the flimsy cover of the ice box. Grunting with effort, he peered into the tiny compartment only to discover what looked like an iceberg, frilled around the edges with frosted particles imported from a winter wonderland.

'*Joder*,' he muttered, reaching for a knife with which to attack the frozen wastes. He stabbed and jabbed and managed to chip out a sizeable chunk, which slid straight out of the box, down onto the tiled floor and broke into several pieces. José closed all the various fridge doors, bent down to retrieve the ice and, throwing it into his untouched drink, smiled at the satisfying sound of the frozen fragments chinking against glass. Lowering himself, at last, to the edge of the chair, he noticed some blood on his hand and realized he must have cut himself during his frenzied attack on the gleaming contents of the weirdly elongated oval-shaped freezer. He pulled a dirty handkerchief out of one of his pockets and wrapped it around the wound on his right thumb.

Now, fully organized and with everything at his fingertips, contentment was complete. José leaned against the back of the rickety chair and gazed at the tranquil world outside the open front door. Suffused in yellow candlelight, the patio seemed soft and gentle, a place for quiet reflection and reconciled dogs. The occasional chirruping from a distant gathering of cicadas formed a pleasant accompaniment to José's meandering thoughts. After several mouthfuls of the sweet sticky

229

liqueur, his mind returned to the wonders of the universe, the stars and the force that held it all together. Sitting in the peace of the darkened timeless kitchen, he wallowed in the warmth emanating from the patio tucked safely into the confines of its enclosing wall.

The atmosphere shattered and collapsed when a jet screamed into the sleeping velvet sky, the sound of protesting engines scraping across the intransigent mountain as the aircraft decelerated towards its seaward starboard swing and eventual rendezvous with Málaga.

José stood up and walked onto the patio, and as he watched the aircraft blinking its way through the night, his mind was transported to the American drama and the pictures he would never forget, *could* never forget; the images of men and women, ordinary everyday men and women scrabbling at thin air with nothing but furious hellfire on every level and an unknown eternal void below. He wondered how God, his God, the tricksy Christian Judge of all men, could have condoned such a wanton act of death and destruction. Then, considering it from the other point of view, he wondered how the other God, the fearless champion of the all-conquering Muslim extremists would explain *His* purpose, *His* helping hand, *His* grand design? A Catholic, born and raised, José had managed to stay clear of the church's beckoning portal since stepping out of it on the day of his wedding, but still he had his opinions. He closed his eyes and understood precisely the whole shabby sanctimonious deal, religion's empty promise of eternal forgiveness and the misconstrued ideals of belief.

'What God?' he asked himself. A snouty friend raised its head but gave no answer.

'What God?' he yelled at the cold silent stars.

And at that moment José realized there *was* no God. How could there be? No one had come bouncing out of celestial incandescence to guide the world in its time of need. Where were they, the righteous Ones, the Allahs and Elohim, the Yahwehs, Jehovahs and Krishnas? Which heavenly sport or television programme was so absorbing that it left no time for divine intervention? Where was the Alpha and the Omega, the Almighty All-holy All-merciful God of everything, the Supreme Being, Creator and Preserver? Where was He, the person with a string of names as diverse as Paco, Pedro and Snow White? All these names, all these gods and all these humans – all different yet one and the same; too many empyrean cooks anointing the sacred broth.

'*Joder*,' José grumbled. 'How many architects does it take to give birth to a universe?'

And the question caused another idea to swim through José's troubled mind. If the person in charge was supposed to be so incredibly powerful, so incredibly in control, why did there have to be so many duplicates? Surely one top dog, one super chef, was sufficient? And, in José's reasoning, this is where the whole design fell to pieces. Either there was one singularity, which José thought probable, possibly; or there was a multitude of omnipresences, all performing the same wondrous magic. Either, or. That there were so many religions, all with the same belief but not really, not in the real world, made the whole thing unbalanced and impossible. Supremely, they cancelled themselves out of the equation. Supremely, they were the cause of more death and more suffering than all of mankind's other devious inventions put together.

José smiled. And then he recalled his earlier take on the

subject, his moment of epiphany, when he'd told María that she and Antonio Banderas were God and that in every beating heart there resides an echo of human goodness.

Sublime in their indifference to the microscopic planet and its self-induced problems and the philanthropic meanderings of an elderly Spaniard, the cold stars regarded José with complete detachment. And while a mosquito zipped menacingly about his head, José withdrew his vision from the cosmos and all its thrilling possibilities and refocused on the aircraft as it angled out of the heavens, its landing lights reaching for the relative safety of the runway.

'Humanity,' José muttered, rocking back-and-forth on his heels, 'it just needs tweaking, a little here and a little there. We can do it ourselves, internally, each one of us, individually and not subject to the whims of a super-deity.'

He closed the door on the subject and went to bed.

As soon as José's head touched the pillow, sleep became a distant reality. He lay on his back and listened to the soft caress of María's safe comfortable breathing coming from the other bed. He lay on his back and stared at the invisible ceiling, at clouds of imagination shifting uneasily in the darkness. Small black dots appeared from nowhere and then a brilliant white light filled his eyes and changed everything. The dots became strange colourful shapes and José saw himself walking through the ceiling into a mysterious forest of tall pine trees, real pine trees, and there in an outstretched hand was the eye of an octopus. José rubbed his eyelids to clear his vision, and yes, the hand belonged to Sebastián, his best friend, in whose sweaty palm were the rings, sparkling rings shimmering just out of reach above the ripples of a wide lake. Dancing pearls of light came falling out of the ceiling, grains of rice, landing, bouncing at the feet of a woman, María, as she raised a veil from her sweet angelic face and revealed a halo, radiant, centred on her left eye, all-seeing, all-knowing, expanding to become a giant Ferris wheel which, at José's command, stopped rotating. Someone was waving at him from behind a swirling curtain of long dark luxuriant hair, weaving sinuously, randomly, as though under water, fashioning images of Jaime and a young girl hiding her face, while a woman dressed in black stood watching and waiting on the platform. 'Hold on to Laia,' the voice, his grandmother's, screamed through the noise of a pumping hurdy-gurdy, 'you're losing her!' A gondola swung lethargically across the flat yellow face of a summer moon, and the girl had vanished.

José lay quietly in the darkness, staring at the invisible ceiling. He was tired, so tired, but his mind was too busy, too vibrantly hectic to allow the luxury of sleep. He lay on his back in the small bedroom and wondered about all these . . . memories? Dreams? He found it strange to be thinking about the past, remembering it as clearly as . . . yesterday.

Sunlight scratched around the ill-fitting curtain and filled the room with morning's golden promise. José opened an eye and tried to decide if he was awake or on yet another of his strange journeys through time. He rolled over to look at the alarm clock and swallowed rapidly as an acrid taste of liquor spilled out of his throat and burned his taste buds.

'María,' he called, idly wondering why she hadn't drawn back the curtains. His head fell back onto the pillow and the room halted its wild gyrations. And then he realized what the clock had told him: ten-twenty! What the hell was she up to?

Why hadn't she come to wake him, and where was his breakfast?

'*¡Joder!*' he exclaimed, sitting up, but not too quickly. He followed the automatic routine of swinging his legs over the side of the bed and searching for back-to-front slippers. Mid belly-scratch, he paused and listened. Nothing. José twisted to the right and shoved his best ear forward; nothing, still nothing. He shook his head and burped at the onset of another attack from last night's acquaintance with the bottle. Feet in slippers, he elevated himself into an aching semi-erect standing position, farting with the exertion of movement.

'María,' he called. 'Where's my breakfast?'

He collected his stick from its night-time resting place against the chair at the side of his bed and hobbled along the dim narrow corridor towards the front door. Opening it, he urged himself through the dazzlingly bright rectangle and took several moments to come to terms with the world outside. The old familiar rumble of the Landrover caused him to squeeze his eyes and squint across the valley, and sure enough there it was, the dirty-white toy vehicle pulling clouds of dust behind it.

'Now what does he want?' he enquired of the comatose dogs. He looked affectionately at his favourite, Blanca, the bitch with the lumpy growth on her belly. 'There's no peace around here,' he confided to the sleeping animal before turning to plod back into the cool interior. 'No peace at all.'

José ran some water into the kettle and switched it on. He couldn't understand what had happened to María and he wasn't too familiar with the way things worked in the kitchen, so he spent time searching for the coffee and then, looking at the kettle, noticed that it hadn't yet boiled. He took a mug from the shelf, put a heaped teaspoon of coffee into it and another half-teaspoon for good luck, and still the kettle hadn't boiled.

'Bloody thing,' he grumbled, and automatically bringing María into the equation, decided it was her fault and blamed her missing persona. 'Stupid woman,' he lamented. 'How many times have I told her to clean the bloody thing? Women, they just don't understand.'

With perfect timing and in response to José's outburst, the kettle switched itself off and sat, hugely smug, gushing steam into the corner of the kitchen. José hefted it from its stand and poured hot water onto the granules, then, remembering he'd just witnessed Vicente and his faithful chariot hurtling along the track, set about preparing a second cup and heaped sugar into both. He stood for a moment, staring vacantly at a pearly drip clinging with measured determination to the lip of the cold tap, and wondered what to do. And then he remembered he'd forgotten to pee. He always peed, every morning; it was the first thing he did. Christ, he thought, how could I forget to pee? And then realized he'd bypassed the normal activity when María, damn the woman, hadn't responded to his call. He looked at the two mugs of coffee, sighed, headed for the bathroom and became aware that, save for his slippers, he was naked. Well, bollocks, he thought, I don't need clothes to pee.

José opened the bathroom door and saw María sitting on the lavatory, voluminous bloomers around her ankles. Hastily, he closed the door.

'¡Venga Venga!' he cried. 'A man needs to pee.' Then, 'How long have you been in there? Christ, woman, I was beginning to think I'd have to get my own breakfast.'

Suddenly, José's need to urinate became a threatening thing of vengeance. He cupped himself in both hands and kicked at the door. 'Come on,' he ordered. 'Hurry *up.*'

Shuffling his feet in uncomfortable anguish, he found himself facing the radiance streaming through the open front door. 'Jesus!' José scrunched his eyes against the brilliant white light and at the edge of sensibility, divined the muted roar of the Landrover. He turned and gave the door another kick. 'María, I need to go, now, before Vicente gets here,' he squawked at the door, voice rising in panic. 'María!'

Again, José kicked at the door, harder, more urgently, and the door flew open and María was still sitting there, resplendently regal.

'For God's sake, woman, get off the toilet!' José screamed. 'I can't wait.'

It was always the way – when he wanted to pee, he couldn't, and when he had to wait, he couldn't do that either; another good reason for questioning the existence of God.

José started to urinate, he couldn't help it, his ancient muscles had betrayed him. Bow-legged, he rushed to the lavatory, grabbed María's shoulders and tried to dislodge her from her imperial arrangement. María fell forward and then fell further forward and José couldn't understand why and didn't know whether to hold himself or hold María. The noise of the Landrover was becoming louder and louder and José couldn't stop peeing and even when the straining engine reached a crescendo and then, suddenly, was switched off, José's decrepit valve remained obstinately open. He lunged forward and grappled with María's slumped body, hoisting it up to rest against the cool white cistern and when their heads met, he looked into her face and saw how white it was, white and translucent and sort of gleaming, shiny like porcelain. María's left hand, free of muscular or cerebral intervention, slithered from her lap and fell to the floor, fingers unfurling bracken-like as though releasing life's misunderstood secrets and its tenuous hold on being; stilled, silent and empty. Reaching out to gather the functionless limb, José caught sight of something crude and dark cradled in María's forgiving palm. Watery eyes peered at the lump of rock, dead but not dead, a crimson filigree of energy, life, shining from a distant universe. Picking it up, he hurled the failed talisman across the room, a thousand memories and a handful of dreams accompanying its flight until they sailed into a gaudy virgin Mary nailed to the wall, and shattered. And then there were footsteps clomping across the tiles of the sun-filled patio and José listened to them, and with the footsteps he heard a voice, Vicente's, the voice of their baby child.

'Papi,' it said. 'Papi, I thought you'd like to come and help turn on the water.' The voice and the footsteps were in the corridor. 'And mama should come with us,' Vicente continued, 'and we can go somewhere for lunch and celebrate.'

A shadow came floating around the corner, preceeding Vicente into the bathroom. 'Today, papi, remember? It's Mamas' birthday.'

Glossary of Spanish words and phrases as used in *Echoes of Andalucía*

Chapter 1: Civil War

1 *p9 jamon* - ham, usually haunch

2 *p15 churros* - type of fritter, sausage-shaped, sugary and sweet. Usually dipped into hot chocolate or coffee.

3 *p19 Joder* - Damn it. (Hurled abusively, it's the equivalent of 'fuck!')

Chapter 2: Breakfast

4 *p30 cortijo* - farmhouse; small, brick-built, whitewashed country cottage

5 *p37 Siéntense* - Sit down

6 *p38 Joder mujer* - Bloody hell, woman

Chapter 3: Beach

7 *p44 ¡Venga venga!* - Come on, come on!

8 *p47 nada* - nothing.

9 *p54 ¡Eh, coño!* - Hey, pest/pain in the ass/troublemaker! – and various other connotations. (A familiarity)

10 *p54 ¿Qué pasa?* - What's happening?

Chapter 3: Beach (Cont.)

11 *p57 'Dame cuatro cañas, cuatro ponches y un agua, cuatro de pez espada, un lenguado, una rosada a la plancha, dos gambas pil-pil y cuatro platitos de patatas fritas.'*

'Give me four beers, four Ponches (liqueurs) and a water, four sword-fish, one sole, one white fish, two *gambas pil-pil* (prawns in hot oil with garlic and chillies) and four plates of chips.'

12 *p57 ¿Y tú, qué tal?* - 'How's it going with you?'

13 *p58 pimientos de Padrón* - Peppers from Padrón (northern Spain). These are small peppers, shaped like chillies. Also referred to as *'One bites, the other doesn't'*, meaning that you will occasionally come across a pepper that is VERY HOT!

Chapter 4: Mid-Morning

14 *p66 Buenos* - Good. (In the context of the story, it's a short-ened form of *Buenos dias* - Good morning. Typical in Andalucían dialect, where many words are cut almost in half!)

Chapter 5: *Feria* (Fair)

15 *p75 Feria* - Fair: a big yearly occasion with funfair, food stalls, live music and shows. Every city, town and village has its own feria.

16 *p76 campo* - countryside

17 *p76 desayuno* - breakfast

18 *p77 pitufos* - small bread rolls

19 *p81 señoritas* - young ladies, girls.

20 *p82 'Mira, un regalo para tí'* - 'Look, a present for you.'

Chapter 5: (Cont.) *Feria* (Fair)

21 *p83 chorizo* - pork sausage, salami.

22 *p83 salchichón* - sausage, salami.

23 *p90 ¡Mierda!* - Shit!

24 *p90 hijo de puta* - bastard. (Literally: son of a prostitute)

Chapter 6: Lunch

25 *p97 Furie* - Roman and Greek Mythology: *Furies* - feared avenging goddesses, relentless tormentors

26 *p98 Niño* - Son. *Niño* also means youngster (term of endearment).

27 *p98 'No te preocupes,'* - 'Don't worry about it.'

28 *p99 ayuntamiento* - Town Hall

29 *p101 Junta* - Council.

30 *p110 'Mañana, mañana; siempre mañana,'* - 'Tomorrow, tomorrow; always tomorrow.'

31 *p110 ¡Joder! ¿Mujer, qué pasa contigo?* - Bloody hell! Woman, what's the matter with you?

Chapter 7: *Enriqueta*

32 *p118 ¿De qué vas?* - What's the matter with you?

33 *p118 ¡Cállate!* - 'Shut up!'

34 *p119 ¡Salud!* - 'Cheers!'

35 *p125 Puchero* - Cooking pot, saucepan or casserole.

36 *p128 ¿José, qué haces?* - 'José, what are you doing?'

37 *p128 'Nada papa. No hago nada.'* - 'Nothing dad. I'm not doing anything.'

Chapter 8: Afternoon

Chapter 9: Wedding

Chapter 10: Interlude

Chapter 11: *Semana Santa* (Holy Week)

Chapter 11: (Cont.) *Semana Santa* (Holy Week)

48 *p181* *'Mira'* - 'Look.'

49 *p181* *Cofrada* - Large hall enclosed by huge doors, home to the local community's Virgin Mary

50 *p182* *¿Y ahora, qué?'* - 'Now what?'

51 *p183* *Caña* - Small glass of beer

Chapter 13: Honeymoon

52 *p198* *¿Dónde estamos?* - Where are we?

53 *p199* *¿Qué?* - What?

54 *p202* *'Magia'* - 'Magic.'

55 *p203* *El dueño* - The owner/proprietor.

56 *p203* *'Sí, sí, señor, estupendo, y tenéis suerte.'* - 'Yes, yes, Sir, wonderful, and you're in luck.'

57 *p204* *¿Cómo estáis?* - 'How are you?' (Plural)

58 *p216* *flans* - crème caramels.

59 *p216* *¿Por qué no?* - 'Why not?'

Chapter 14: Dreams

60 *p225* *Dama del Noche* - (Lady of the Night)
Heavily sweet- scented climbing plant. Especially fragrant in the evening and at night-time. (Latin: *Cestrum nocturnum*)

61 *p227* *¡Fuera!* - Get out! Go away!

62 *p227* *morcilla* - blood sausage; black pudding

63 *p228* *por fin* - finally; at last

R i p p l e s

Richard C Pizey

Alex and Jessica live in north London and, like many young
couples, lead a problematic life. Now, unbidden, an extra
dimension lands on the doormat and adds to their troubles.

Set in the 1980s, this ingenious story flirts with humour,
music, art history, Nazi machination . . . and sex, as Alex and
Jessica delve into the secrets behind a set of paintings recently
discovered in upstate New York.
Linking past to present and attempting to unravel the intricacies of art fraud, this whirlwind adventure combines mystery
and intimacy and hurtles through London, New York, Bavaria
and Scotland on a quest concerned not only with works of
art, but also with the struggles of an in-your-face relationship.

Bold, brash and upfront, *Ripples* tantalizes, teases and trans-
ports you to places and situations previously confined to your
imagination.

Ripples is the first novel from Richard C Pizey, and is available
from bookshops or at www.augmentedfifth.com

AUGMENTED FIFTH
ANOTHER DIMENSION
www.augmentedfifth.com

R i p p l e s